MW01596430

Books By
Joab Stieglitz

The Utgarda Series
The Old Man's Request
The Missing Medium
The Other Realm
The Hunter in the Shadows:
The Worlds I Know

Agent of the Overlords Series
Designed for Slaughter
Bound for Duty
The Crucible of Control

The Crucible of Control

Agent of the Overlords #3

Joab Stieglitz

CHAPTER 1

Larry Nodens lay on the couch in the living room of his small apartment, his body adorned with bandages, a testament to the injuries he had sustained during his last harrowing case. Sunlight streamed in through the expansive floor-to-ceiling windows behind him, casting long shadows on the furniture. Despite the brightness outside, his mood remained somber and distant, weighed down by a heavy burden.

It had been three long weeks since the fateful encounter at the Temple of the Yellow Sign, a place steeped in eldritch horrors and forbidden knowledge. Larry, accompanied by his goth second-in-command Farley and his courageous daughter Dani, had faced off against the malevolent Cult of the Yellow Sign. Their combined efforts, bolstered by the timely intervention of the enigmatic Black Watchmen, a group of vigilant protectors of the aquatic Children of Dagon, had managed to thwart the cult's sinister plans. Together, they had prevented an unnamed Old One from manifesting in the city of Dylath-Leen who could have challenged the very rule of the Overlords themselves.

But victory had come at a cost. Larry and Farley bore flensing wounds inflicted by the tentacles of their unearthly adversaries. A figure in a white suit, their face hidden behind a welding helmet, had come to their aid, searing away the writhing appendages that threatened to consume them. Now, the bandages enshrouding their limbs served as a reminder of the physical toll exacted by their encounter, even as their bodies slowly healed.

Larry's physical discomfort was secondary to the anguish that gripped his heart. Thoughts of his beloved daughter Dani consumed his every waking moment. In the midst of the battle, the cultists had ruthlessly carved forbidden symbols into her tender flesh, causing her to lose a dangerous amount of blood. Although she had played a pivotal role in the defeat of the Old One, her bravery had come at a great cost.

The Overlords had intervened. Just as they had taken Larry's wife, Charlotte, twelve years prior, they had now claimed Dani. Charlotte, Selected by the Overlords, had been whisked away to an unknown fate. Larry was left to grieve and question, forever unsure of her whereabouts. But this time, with Dani, it was different. Larry knew the location of his daughter's captivity—the Schola.

Locked down since the incident, the training academy for future citizens of the Overlord regime had become an impenetrable fortress. Larry's efforts, which included leveraging his network and authority as an inspector, proved futile against the Overlords' iron grip on the institution. He felt powerless, trapped in a web of bureaucracy and secrecy that separated him from his daughter.

The couch beneath Larry's weary body offered little comfort. His bandaged limbs were a painful, constant reminder of what he'd been through. He yearned for Dani's presence, her voice, and the reassurance that she was safe.

Despite the sunlight streaming in through the windows, the room remained veiled in darkness. The gloomy mood really mirrored how Larry was feeling, showing the inner chaos he was going through. He knew he had to find a way to reach Dani. He had to get her home safely, but the road ahead was unclear.

¤

As Larry's memories of Dani flooded his mind, the weight of their separation bore down on him like an impenetrable darkness. He clutched his bandaged chest.

Dani had always been a beacon of light in Larry's life, a constant source of joy and inspiration. He cherished their moments together, from the countless conversations they had shared, to the fierce pride he felt as he watched her excel at the Schola. Her determination and resilience had always impressed him, and he had believed that she would navigate the treacherous path of the Schola with her characteristic strength.

Larry's mind drifted back to the last time Dani had donned her Schola uniform, adorned with ribbons and symbols of her achievements. The sight of her standing tall and confident had filled him with a mixture of pride and sorrow. The happy memories were tinged with the sadness of knowing their time together wouldn't last. The Overlords were absolute rulers, dictating not only how the people lived but also how they would meet their end.

Nothing could have prepared Larry for the abruptness with which the Overlords had taken Dani from him. The six months they had planned to spend together before her obligatory service were cut short by what happened at the old temple below the Kuttner Sanitorium. The Overlords' interference cast a shadow over their lives.

They were supposed to have had six more months together before Dani left for her mandatory service. Six months to say a proper goodbye and reconnect, hoping she would return someday. But now she was gone. Out of his reach. He hadn't heard from Dani since the Overlords took her.

Larry hadn't heard from Dani since that terrible day, and he was completely lost without knowing how she was. The Overlords had effectively cut off all communication, leaving him adrift in a sea of uncertainty. The anguish of not knowing consumed him, amplifying his fears and fueling his determination to find a way to reach his daughter once more.

¤

Larry sat alone, remembering Dani as a sweet, innocent little girl.

He remembered her bright, curious eyes, always filled with a spark of excitement as she explored the world around her. From the moment she took her first steps, Larry watched with a mixture of pride and trepidation as Dani fearlessly ventured into new territories, eager to discover what lay beyond her grasp.

Larry reminisced about the countless hours spent having tea parties, building towering block forts, and reading bedtime stories with Dani tucked safely in his arms. Each memory was etched deep within his heart, a precious collection of moments that he cherished more than anything in the world.

He recalled the sound of Dani's laughter, pure and infectious, echoing through the walls of their home. Her giggles were like music, a melody that brought joy to even the darkest of days. Larry could almost feel her tiny arms wrapped around his neck, the warmth of her breath against his cheek as she whispered, "I love you, Daddy."

In his memories, Larry saw Dani's face light up with awe and wonder as she discovered new things. From the simple beauty of a flower in bloom to the vast expanse and always changing night sky, her capacity to find joy in the smallest of moments was a constant reminder of the beauty in life.

He remembered the nights when he would sit by Dani's bedside, reading her favorite stories until her eyelids grew heavy. The softness of her breathing, the peacefulness that washed over her as sleep claimed her, brought a sense of calm and fulfillment to Larry's soul.

As he allowed himself to dive deeper into the memories, Larry recalled the challenges they faced together. The scraped knees and tears that required his comforting embrace, the nights when fears and nightmares threatened to overwhelm her young spirit.

Through it all, he stood as her rock, providing love, support, and reassurance.

But time had a way of slipping through his fingers, and Larry couldn't stop it from carrying them forward. His daughter was no longer the wide-eyed child. She had grown into a strong, young woman, facing her own set of challenges and discoveries.

And though the years had transformed Dani into a young adult, Larry knew that the essence of who she was, the spirit that had blossomed within her as a child, would forever be a part of her. He would carry those memories in his heart, a beacon of light in the moments when he missed the little girl she once was.

With a gentle smile on his face, Larry whispered into the stillness of the room, "You've grown so much, my dear Dani. But no matter where life takes you, know that you will always be my little girl, and my love for you will never fade."

CHAPTER 2

The buzz of the doorbell roused Larry from his thoughts.

"Just a minute," he said as he stiffly rose from the couch. Despite the bandages restricting his movement, he managed to shuffle towards the front door. Peeking through the peephole, Larry saw the smiling faces of Gwen Pabodie and Alan Gilman. Gwen was holding their daughter, Tabitha, and Alan was carrying some grocery bags.

Larry unlocked and opened the door.

"Hey, Larry! How are you feeling?" Gwen greeted him cheerfully, her eyes filled with genuine concern. Alan nodded, a warm smile on his face.

Larry forced a smile, appreciating their visit. "I'm hanging in there," he replied, stepping aside to let them into his apartment. He closed the door behind them, leaning against it for support.

Alan observed the gloomy living room, his attention drawn to Larry's injured body. "We brought some groceries for you," he said, holding up the bags. "We figured you could use a break from takeout."

Gwen chimed in, her voice filled with empathy. "And we brought little Tabitha to brighten your day. Babies have a magical way of bringing smiles, you know?"

Larry's somber expression softened as he looked at the adorable bundle in Gwen's arms. Tabitha yawned and blinked her innocent eyes, oblivious to the darkness that overshadowed Larry's life. The sight brought a flicker of warmth to his heart.

"That's really kind of you both," Larry replied, stepping forward to get a closer look at Tabitha. He gently touched her tiny hand, marveling at its delicate perfection. It reminded him of the fragility of life and the importance of protecting those we love.

Alan placed the grocery bags on the kitchen counter, turning back to Larry.

"We're here for you, Larry. We know it's been tough since Dani... since everything happened," Gwen said.

Alan nodded in agreement. "You're not alone in this, Sir. We're your friends, and we'll support you however we can."

A surge of gratitude welled up within Larry as he looked at the couple before him. They had been there for him through thick and thin, and their unwavering friendship meant the world to him. He knew he couldn't face his challenges alone, and their presence gave him strength.

"Thank you," Larry said, his voice sincere. "I don't know what I would do without you two."

Gwen smiled, reaching out to give Larry a reassuring pat on the arm. "You don't have to worry about that, Larry. We'll get through this together."

Gwen's words rekindled Larry's hope. He realized that even in the darkest of times, there were people who cared about him and were willing to offer their support. The weight of his burdens seemed a little lighter, and a spark of determination ignited within him.

In the kitchen, Gwen and Alan began unpacking the groceries, taking charge of organizing and preparing a homemade meal. Larry watched them in awe, grateful for their thoughtfulness and the comforting normality they brought into his life.

Tabitha, nestled in a soft blanket, was placed into her carrier on the floor. Larry, still mindful of his injuries, settled onto the couch nearby, where he could keep an eye on her. The soft coos and gurgles that escaped her tiny lips created a soothing ambiance, providing a brief respite from the troubles that plagued Larry's mind.

The friends enjoyed a lively conversation as the delicious smell of home-cooked food wafted through the apartment. Gwen and Alan caught Larry up on their personal lives, sharing stories and jokes that made everyone in the room laugh. During that time, Larry had a taste of normalcy, even if it was brief.

Between bites of the delicious meal, Larry found himself

opening up about his emotions and the challenges he faced since the incident. He shared his struggles with the physical pain, the haunting memories, and the uncertainty of what lay ahead. Gwen and Alan listened intently, their eyes filled with compassion and understanding.

"You're a fighter, Larry," Gwen whispered, her voice full of belief. "I've seen you go through tough times, and you always bounce back stronger."

Alan nodded in agreement, his expression supportive. "We believe in you, Sir. You have the courage to overcome this."

Their words resonated deeply within Larry, reinforcing his determination to heal and move forward. In the midst of his pain and uncertainty, he found solace in the unwavering support of his friends. They reminded him that he was not defined by his scars or his past, but by his resilience and the love he had for those who mattered most.

As the evening drew to a close, and the last remnants of dinner were cleared away, Gwen and Alan prepared to leave. Larry accompanied them to the door, a genuine smile now adorning his face.

"Thank you again for everything," Larry said, his voice filled with gratitude. "You've reminded me of the strength I have within me, and I can't express how much your support means to me."

Gwen hugged him tightly. "Remember, Larry, we're just a phone call away. Anytime you need to talk or if you need help with anything."

Alan shook Larry's hand firmly, his eyes reflecting unwavering support. "Stay strong, my friend. You have the power to write your own future. Take one step at a time, and don't hesitate to lean on us when you need it."

As Larry closed the door behind them, a newfound sense of hope filled his heart. Though the road to recovery would be long and challenging, he knew he didn't have to face it alone. With the support of his friends and the strength he discovered within himself, he was ready to embark on the journey toward healing and a brighter future.

¤

Turning away from the door, Larry walked back into the living room. The sun was setting, casting a warm, orange glow through the windows. He paused for a moment, allowing the peaceful ambiance to wash over him.

He was just about to lie down on the couch again when there was a labored knock on the door.

Larry hobbled back and looked through the peephole. The huge form of his partner, Horace Whately, stood there, holding a small keg of Pnakotic Ale. Larry quickly unlocked the door and opened it.

"Hello, Sir!" Horace greeted him with a wide grin, his deep voice booming through the doorway. "I come bearing the finest Pnakotic Ale in Dylath-Leen. Figured you could use a taste of something good after all you've been through."

Larry's weariness momentarily lifted as he returned Horace's smile. He stepped aside, allowing his partner to enter the apartment. "You read my mind, Horace. A drink sounds like just what the doctor ordered."

Horace made his way to the living room, carefully placing the keg on the coffee table. Larry did the same and carefully sat down on the couch, his injured body appreciating the comfort. He couldn't help but chuckle at the sight of the keg, a glimmer of anticipation flickering in his eyes.

With practiced ease, Horace produced two frosted glasses from his bag and tapped the keg, filling them with the amber liquid. He handed one glass to Larry, raising his own in a toast. "To overcoming challenges and finding the truth."

The sweet, malty aroma of Pnakotic Ale filled the room, tickling Larry's nostrils. The rich, nutty scent of the liquid permeated the air, comforting him like an old blanket.

Larry clinked his glass against Horace's, a sense of camaraderie washing over him. "To finding the truth," he echoed, before taking a long sip of the Pnakotic Ale. The smooth, rich flavors danced across his palate, momentarily transporting him away from the weight of his troubles.

As Larry and Horace sat there savoring their drinks, the room filled with an air of familiarity and comfort. Horace's presence, with his larger-than-life personality, had a way of easing the burden on Larry's shoulders. It was a reminder of the bond they shared and the countless cases they had tackled together.

Horace leaned forward, his eyes narrowing as he recalled a particular case. "Remember that murder in Old Dylath? The victim's body was torn apart, just like the signature of a Ravager. Everyone thought one had crossed over again."

Larry nodded, his mind drifting back to the intricate investigation they had undertaken. "Yes, I remember. The panic was palpable. But as we dug deeper, we realized it wasn't Ravagers. It was a cleverly orchestrated ruse by a human killer, using their M.O. to throw us off."

Horace's voice lowered, filled with a mix of admiration and frustration. "The way they replicated the Ravagers' methods... it was chilling. But we saw through the deception. Together, we unraveled the truth and brought the real culprit to justice."

Their shared memories intertwined, each case a testament to their perseverance and deductive skills. They had encountered numerous instances where murderers capitalized on the fear surrounding the Ravagers to conceal their own heinous acts.

Larry sat back, looking thoughtful. "And what about that series of killings in Oriab? The locals were convinced it was the work of Ravagers, but we knew better."

Horace's eyes gleamed with pride. "Absolutely! We studied the patterns and realized the true nature of those murders. It wasn't those interdimensional predators, but a disturbed individual who had harnessed the fear of the supernatural to sow chaos and cover their tracks."

They had tirelessly unraveled the complex puzzle of evidence, working through countless sleepless nights. With adrenaline pumping through their veins, they boldly confronted the perpetrators, refusing to back down in their relentless pursuit of justice. Every case was a trial of their strength and resilience, but their steadfast dedication to uncovering the truth always triumphed, despite interference from Agent Oikos and the RATF.

They recalled their most memorable victories. It was moments like these that made all the hard work and danger worth it.

Larry's voice grew resolute. "Those cases taught us something important, Horace. The Ravagers might be a formidable threat from another dimension, but we can't let their presence blind us to the human evil that lurks within our own world. We must remain vigilant and discerning."

Horace nodded in agreement, a fire burning in his eyes. "You're right, Sir. We can't afford to be swayed by fear or assumptions. We owe it to the victims and their families to seek justice, whether the culprit is human or something otherworldly."

As they continued to reminisce, their determination grew, solidifying their commitment to uncover the truth, no matter how deep the shadows may run. United by their shared past, Larry and Horace were prepared to confront any mysteries that lay before them, their bond unyielding and their dedication unshakable.

Hours passed, the conversation flowing effortlessly, until both men found themselves nearing the end of the keg. Larry's exhaustion began to creep back in, his body reminding him of the need for rest.

Horace stood up, stretching his arms above his head. "Well, my friend, I should be heading out. But remember, Sir, you're not alone in this. We've faced worse odds before, and we'll face them again. Together."

Larry nodded, gratitude shining in his eyes. "Thank you, Horace. Your friendship means the world to me. I'll never forget that."

As Horace made his way towards the door, Larry couldn't help but feel a renewed sense of determination. He knew the road ahead would be treacherous, filled with uncertainty and danger. But with a team like Horace, Gwen, and Alan by his side, he had the strength to face whatever challenges lay ahead.

Closing the door behind Horace, Larry made his way back to the couch, ready to rest and gather his energy for the journey ahead. As he settled in, the remnants of the Pnakotic Ale warming his veins, he allowed himself a small smile.

CHAPTER 3

Larry woke up to a gentle shake of his shoulder. He opened his eyes to find Farley leaning over him with a concerned expression. She had a key to the apartment but had been staying at her own place since the incident.

Both Larry and Farley were bandaged, but Farley's athletic physique allowed her more mobility compared to Larry's older frame. Her short brown hair framed her face, which was adorned with goth makeup. As always, she wore a black studded leather collar around her neck, although she had opted for loose sweatpants and a v-neck t-shirt instead of her usual skin-tight wardrobe.

"Did you sleep on the couch again?" she asked, her concern evident.

Larry carefully sat up, feeling his stiff muscles protest, and turned his head from side to side to relieve a kink in his neck. Farley moved behind him and began massaging his neck with her warm hands.

"You should sleep in the bed. You won't get proper rest on the couch," she advised.

Larry grinned wearily. "Why don't you stay and make sure I do what's good for me?"

"I'm here to start your training. The Overlords are waiting to evaluate you," Farley replied.

Exhaustion and anticipation filled Larry as he remembered the evaluation and his need to find Dani.

"Right," Larry replied, his voice tinged with resignation. "The evaluation. I suppose we can't keep them waiting."

Farley's hands paused, and she stepped back, concern etched across her features. "Larry, I know this is difficult for you. But remember, this evaluation is crucial. It's your chance to prove yourself, to show the Overlords that you can handle what lies ahead."

Nodding, Larry acknowledged her words. "I understand, Farley. It's just... everything that has happened—losing Dani, the cult, the injuries... It's hard to focus sometimes."

Placing a reassuring hand on his shoulder, Farley offered a comforting squeeze. "I know it's overwhelming. But you have been chosen by the Overlords to take these examinations. You have proven yourself worthy of the chance to work for them."

With her help, Larry was able to get up from the couch and motioned towards the bedroom. "Alright, let's go. I'll get some rest before the evaluation."

As they made their way to the bedroom, Farley glanced at him with a faint smile. "And don't worry, I'll make sure you actually sleep in the bed this time. No couch for you."

He weakly chuckled, grateful for her determination and concern. They entered the room, and Larry carefully settled onto the bed, mindful of his injuries. Farley pulled the covers over him, tucking him in with a gentle touch.

"Just relax," she said softly, her voice soothing. "Clear your mind and focus on getting some much-needed rest. We'll face the evaluation together when you're ready."

Larry closed his eyes, allowing Farley's words to guide him toward a state of tranquility. He took a deep breath, feeling the tension slowly dissipate. The events of the past weeks began to fade into the background as he embraced the peacefulness of the present moment.

¤

Larry sat on the edge of Dani's bed, his heart heavy with the burden he was about to place upon his young daughter. Dani, now seven years old, looked up at him with her wide, innocent eyes, unaware of the weight of the words that were about to be spoken. He took a deep breath, trying to gather the strength to share the painful truth.

"Dani, sweetheart," Larry began gently, his voice filled with both sadness and love, "I need to tell you something important about your mother."

Dani tilted her head slightly, her curiosity piqued. "What about Mommy, Daddy? Why isn't she here?"

Larry took a moment to gather his thoughts, searching for the right words to explain the inexplicable. "Dani, your mother was taken by the Overlords."

"The Overlords?" Dani repeated, her voice filled with innocent confusion. "Who are they, Daddy?"

Larry sighed, his eyes filled with memories of the day that changed their lives forever. "The Overlords are powerful beings, Dani. They came to our world, and they decided to take people away without asking. They believed it was their right as rulers."

Dani's eyes widened in shock and fear, her small hand reaching for Larry's. "But... but why did they take Mommy, Daddy?"

Larry gently squeezed her hand, his voice trembling slightly. "I don't know, sweetheart. They didn't give us a reason. They just took her."

Tears welled up in Dani's eyes, her lower lip quivering as the weight of her mother's absence settled upon her small shoulders. "Did Mommy do something wrong, Daddy? Is that why they took her?"

Larry shook his head vehemently, his voice filled with determination. "No, Dani, your mother didn't do anything wrong. It wasn't her fault. The Overlords didn't choose people based on who they were or what they had done. We don't know why they do it."

"Why?" Dani's voice wavered, a mix of sorrow and anger lacing her words. "Why would they do something so mean, Daddy?"

Larry's voice softened, his gaze filled with love and pain. "I wish I had the answers, Dani. I wish I could explain why they did what they did. But what's important to know is that your mother loved you very much. She didn't want to leave us, but she didn't have a choice."

Dani wiped her tears with her small hands, her voice filled with a mix of sadness and determination. "I miss Mommy, Daddy."

Larry wrapped his arms around Dani, pulling her close in a comforting embrace. "I miss her too, sweetheart," he said, a hint of sadness in his voice.

Dani clung to her father tightly, finding solace in his love and warmth. With a gentle kiss on the top of her head, Larry spoke in a voice brimming with adoration and unwavering certainty. "Dani, always remember that there are people who care about you and are there for you, no matter what."

¤

Larry woke up feeling refreshed from a restful sleep, noting that his bandages were still clean, indicating his movements hadn't reopened any wounds. He turned to find Farley lying beside him, watching him with a smile. The thought of intimacy crossed Larry's mind, but the discomfort from his sore muscles quickly made him dismiss it. Farley caressed his face and spoke with a knowing smile.

"There won't be any of that for a while," she said. "At least not until after you complete the examination." She got out of bed, dressed in a short bathrobe. "Do you need help freshening up? The examination starts after breakfast."

Larry appreciated Farley's concern and the reminder of their priorities. He nodded, acknowledging her words. "Thank you, Farley. I could use a hand. The hot water might do wonders for these aching muscles."

Farley extended her hand, helping him out of bed with care. They made their way to the bathroom, and Larry leaned against the counter as Farley adjusted the shower temperature to his liking.

"You have endured a great deal, Sir," she said, her voice reflecting deep understanding. But I know you can handle it.

Meeting her gaze in the mirror, Larry saw the unwavering

support reflected in her eyes. He mustered a smile, grateful for her presence. "Thank you, Farley. I don't know what I would do without you."

Larry undressed with Farley's assistance and removed his bandages. The cascade of water provided a soothing sensation against his tired body as he stepped into the shower, leaning against the wall for support.

Farley handed him a bar of soap, never breaking eye contact. "Take your time, Sir. Let the water ease your tension. Breakfast will be waiting when you're done."

Larry nodded, lathering the soap in his hands. He took a break from his worries, letting the water cleanse him of the troubles of the past weeks. At that moment, he just focused on the present and felt better.

Larry turned off the shower and stepped out, feeling slightly invigorated. Farley handed him a towel, her smile reassuring. He dried himself off carefully. Farley changed his bandages, and Larry dressed in fresh clothes she had laid out.

Ready for the day, he made his way to the kitchen where a simple breakfast spread awaited him. The aroma of freshly brewed coffee filled the air, awakening Larry's senses.

They enjoyed their meal in comfortable silence, nourishing their bodies for the challenges ahead. With each bite, Larry's resolve strengthened, fueled by his love for his daughter and the unwavering support of those who believed in him.

As breakfast concluded, Farley stood up to clear the dishes. Larry reached out, taking her hand and giving it a gentle squeeze. "Thank you, Farley, for everything. I'm ready to face the examination now."

Her warm smile said it all - she was proud. "Don't worry, you've got this.

¤

"Okay," Larry said, his voice filled with anticipation. "What happens now?"

"Now we proceed to the bedroom, and you'll take a seat in your desk chair," Farley replied. "Then we'll begin today's testing sequence."

"The examination will take place here?" Larry asked, seeking clarification.

"It can be conducted anywhere," she explained. "But considering your recovery, it's best for you to stay at home in case of any unforeseen circumstances."

Larry's anxiety surfaced as he asked, "What kind of circumstances?"

"Anything can happen when the Overlords are involved," Farley responded. "The experiences will feel incredibly real, and the consequences will be genuine. I'll be here to monitor you and ensure your physical well-being throughout."

Nodding, Larry followed Farley into the bedroom and settled into the armchair at his desk. To his surprise, Farley strapped his arms to the chair's arms and his legs to the chair's legs.

"We're taking precautions to prevent any potential injuries," she explained, noting Larry's apprehension. She offered him a reassuring grin. "Don't worry. Just focus on what lies ahead. You'll be fine, and I'll be watching over you."

Larry took a deep breath, attempting to calm his nerves as Farley secured the straps. He trusted her implicitly, knowing she had his best interests at heart. While the restraints felt restrictive, he understood their necessity for his safety during the examination.

"Remember, Sir, this evaluation is crucial. The Overlords will be observing, assessing your abilities and potential."

Larry nodded, his gaze fixed on the terminal before him. Obsessed with Dani, their mysterious findings, and the pursuit of the cult and the Old Ones' truth, his mind raced. He knew this crucial exam would help him find his daughter and solve the dangerous mysteries surrounding them.

Farley's voice broke through his contemplation, bringing him back to the present moment. "Are you ready?"

Taking a deep breath, Larry steeled himself. "I'm ready, Farley. Let's do this."

With those words, the room around Larry seemed to dissolve. The familiar surroundings of his apartment faded away, replaced by an ethereal landscape. Visions, fragmented memories, and intricate puzzles materialized before him, each one presenting a challenge to be conquered.

CHAPTER 4

Larry was suddenly transported to a realm where the laws of physics were defied, encountering shifting gravity and blurred dimensions. In a realm of swirling mists that mirrored his inner conflict, he stood, seemingly on another plane of existence. The bandages were no longer present and his body had been restored to its original state.

Larry could sense the weight of his insecurities and doubts pressing against his consciousness, ready to consume him if he faltered. As the mist cleared, a series of interconnected pathways, each leading to a different encounter, were revealed. Each encounter was a test of Larry's resolve and his capacity to distinguish truth from lies.

Larry took a deep breath, trying to steady his racing heart as he surveyed the maze of pathways before him. The air felt heavy, as if it carried the weight of past failures and forgotten dreams. His palms grew clammy, and he anxiously wiped them on his pants. This was not what he had expected.

With trepidation, Larry stepped onto the first pathway, the ground shifting beneath his feet as he moved forward. The surroundings transformed as he progressed, shifting from a desolate forest to a decrepit mansion with twisted corridors. The walls seemed to breathe, whispering haunting secrets that echoed in his ears. Larry's mind raced, questioning whether he was losing his sanity or if this was all part of the test.

As he continued along the path, a sense of unease settled deep within him. Shadows danced in the corners of his vision, taunting him with their elusiveness. His instincts screamed at him to turn back, but something inside him propelled him forward. A mixture of curiosity and apprehension.

The first encounter materialized in front of him—a dimly lit room with a single spotlight illuminating a worn-out chair. A figure sat there, cloaked in darkness, their face hidden from view. Larry's pulse quickened as he approached, the intensity of the situation amplifying his anxiety. The figure spoke, their voice echoing through the chamber.

"Tell me, Lazarus Balthazar Nodens," the figure whispered, their voice a chilling blend of malice and intrigue. "What is the truth behind your deepest regret?"

Larry's mind raced, memories flashing before his eyes like fragments of a shattered mirror. The weight of his past mistakes threatened to crush him. He hesitated, grappling with the fear of exposing his vulnerabilities to this enigmatic figure. But deep down, he knew that confronting his regrets was the only way to move forward.

Summoning his courage, Larry began to unravel the tangled web of emotions that had haunted him for years. He spoke of lost opportunities, broken relationships, and the pain of abandoning his dreams. With each word, the figure seemed to grow more powerful, as if feeding on Larry's anguish.

Once he had poured out his soul, the figure remained silent, their presence an oppressive force in the room. Larry waited, his heart pounding in his chest, unsure of what would come next. A twisted smile slowly formed on the figure's face, and they leaned forward, their eyes gleaming with a mixture of satisfaction and sadistic delight.

"The truth is," the figure hissed, "you will forever be haunted by your regrets. They will consume you, until there is nothing left but a shell of what you once were."

Larry's vision blurred, his head throbbing with a pulsating ache. The weight of his regrets intensified, threatening to suffocate him. Doubts flooded his mind, whispering that he was indeed destined to be trapped in this psychological labyrinth forever.

But somewhere within the depths of his despair, a spark of determination ignited. Larry refused to let his regrets define him. With newfound resolve, he forced himself to move forward, to confront the next challenge that awaited him in this twisted realm.

As Larry walked away from the encounter, the figure's laughter echoed in his ears, a haunting reminder of the torment he would face in the trials to come.

¤

"Sir, are you alright?" Farley asked, her voice filled with concern as she knelt in front of him.

Larry blinked several times, his senses slowly coming back into focus. He was again in his chair. His throat felt dry, making it difficult to speak.

Recognizing his need, Farley held up an opaque bottle with an integrated straw, offering him a drink. Larry eagerly sucked on the straw, feeling the liquid quickly moistening his throat and clearing his mind. He could now fully focus on Farley's presence.

"I feel strange," Larry admitted, his voice still a little hoarse, "but I'll be alright."

Farley nodded, her expression understanding. "Are you able to continue with the testing, or do you need a moment to collect yourself?"

Taking a deep breath, Larry straightened his posture, determination shining in his eyes. "No, I can continue. Let's proceed."

"As you wish," Farley replied, acknowledging his decision.

Larry focused again on the flashing dot on the computer screen.

¤

Larry stood at the foot of a towering mountain. A fog settled on it, obscuring every detail. Larry couldn't make out what lay at the summit. Nor could he see the path leading up to it, or even determine what material made up the mountain's peak.

At the foot of the mountain, Larry could still hear the distant wind buffet against the trees. As he climbed higher, the wind's howling became more pronounced, its cry harmonious with the lonely song of wolves howling in the distance. The howls converged, forming a chilling chorus.

Larry's heart raced as he approached, uncertain of what awaited him at the summit. Doubt whispered in his ear, casting shadows of uncertainty across his path. He steeled himself, reminding himself that the illusions were just manifestations of his own fears.

Larry trudged up the steep slope of the mountain, each step a battle against his own self-doubt. The thick fog enveloped him, obscuring his vision and amplifying the eerie silence that now hung in the air. He strained his ears, hoping to catch any clue or warning that would guide him through this treacherous trial.

As he ascended higher, the air grew thinner, adding a layer of suffocating pressure to his already burdened mind. His legs burned with exertion, but the internal turmoil threatened to overwhelm him far more than the physical strain. Doubt continued to gnaw at him, whispering insidious thoughts of failure and inadequacy.

The fog abruptly parted slightly, revealing a narrow ledge that cut across the face of the mountain. Larry gingerly stepped onto it, the gusty winds threatening to push him off. The ledge looked precarious, its width only sufficient for him to maintain his footing. But he knew he had no choice but to continue, to face whatever lay ahead.

With each cautious step, Larry's doubts grew stronger, morphing into cruel illusions that tormented him relentlessly. Shadows danced along the edge of his vision, whispering malicious lies. He pressed on, his determination fueled by a glimmer of hope that he could conquer his own insecurities.

As he rounded a sharp bend, the fog thickened once more, obscuring the path entirely. Larry felt a wave of despair as anxiety tightened its grip on him. It was as if the mountain itself conspired against him, manipulating his surroundings to further challenge his resolve. But he refused to surrender to the deception.

Taking a deep breath, Larry closed his eyes and focused on his inner strength. He needed to rely on his instincts and trust that he could navigate the illusions. Slowly, he extended his hand, reaching out into the mist. His fingertips grazed something solid, and he grasped onto it, his grip firm and unwavering.

When he opened his eyes, Larry found himself standing on a small platform, suspended high above the abyss. The fog cleared for a moment, revealing a grotesque statue carved from the mountain itself. Its features were twisted, contorted into a terrifying mask of fear and despair. Its hollow eyes seemed to bore into Larry's soul, testing his resolve.

"You cannot escape the depths of your own self-doubt," a voice echoed through the air, emanating from the statue. "You will forever be trapped in this cycle of insecurity and torment."

Larry felt a surge of anger rise within him, a defiance that shattered the chains of doubt that bound him. He had endured too much, faced too many trials, to be defeated now. The statue was just another test, a manifestation of his own fears.

Summoning every ounce of courage he possessed, Larry stepped forward and swung his fist at the statue. The impact shattered the stone, sending fragments cascading into the abyss below. The echoes of the statue's voice faded, replaced by a resounding silence that washed over Larry like a balm.

In that moment, Larry realized that the power to overcome his self-doubt resided within himself. He had the strength to dismantle the illusions that held him captive. No longer would he allow fear to dictate his path.

With renewed determination, Larry pressed forward, leaving behind the shattered remnants of the statue. He knew that the trials were far from over, but he was no longer afraid. The next challenge awaited him, and he was prepared to face it head-on, armed with the knowledge that he possessed the strength to overcome any obstacle that stood in his way.

¤

Larry was taken aback when he returned to reality and noticed Farley bandaging his bruised and slightly bleeding knuckles, despite his arms being firmly strapped to the chair. He looked at her with disbelief written on his face.

"I warned you," she said, her voice tinged with concern. "The experiences during these tests are real. You have to be careful."

As Farley finished wrapping his knuckles, the pain from his injured hands began to show, and Larry quietly cursed.

Once again, Farley brought the bottle to his lips, and Larry took a long drink. The liquid cleared his throat and revived him, but this time it also numbed the pain in his hands.

"I think it's time for a break," she said, loosening the straps that held his arms. "You've done enough for today."

"But we've just begun!" Larry protested.

"You've been in the tests for nearly ten hours. You need to rest," Farley insisted.

As she released his arms and legs from the restraints, Larry realized the extent of his mental and physical exhaustion. He accepted the bottle and held the straw to his lips, finishing its contents.

"Don't worry," Farley reassured him. "There will be more tests tomorrow."

With Farley's help, Larry struggled to rise from the chair, his body feeling stiff and fatigued. She guided him to the bed and helped him lie down, tucking him in under the blankets. Then she joined him on the bed, snuggling up to him as he rested his head on her shoulder.

In a matter of moments, the weariness overtook them both, and they drifted into a peaceful slumber, finding solace in each other's presence.

CHAPTER 5

The morning sunlight spilled through the curtains, casting a warm glow as Larry stood at the doorway of Dani's bedroom. His heart felt heavy with a mix of pride and a tinge of sadness. Dani was leaving for the Schola, embarking on a new chapter of her life.

Taking a deep breath, Larry stepped into the room, finding Dani sitting on her bed in her new uniform, a suitcase beside her. Her eyes were filled with a mixture of excitement and apprehension. Larry couldn't help but feel a pang of nostalgia, knowing that things would never quite be the same.

"Dani," Larry began, his voice tinged with a mix of emotions, "I can't believe how fast time has flown. It feels like just yesterday you were a little girl, and now you're about to embark on this new journey."

Dani looked up at her father, a bittersweet smile on her face. "I know, Dad. It's hard to believe it myself. But I'm ready for this. I'm ready to learn, grow, and explore what the world has to offer."

Larry nodded, his eyes brimming with pride. "I know you are, sweetheart. You're strong, smart, and capable. I have no doubt that you'll thrive at the Schola. But before you go, I want to share something with you."

Curiosity flickered in Dani's eyes as Larry reached into his pocket, pulling out an old, weathered journal. He handed it to her, his voice filled with nostalgia. "This journal belonged to your mother, Dani. She used to write in it when she was young, documenting her dreams, her aspirations, and her hopes for the future."

Dani held the journal in her hands, her fingers tracing the worn pages. "I've heard stories about Mom. She was so brave and kind. I wish I could've known her."

A tender smile graced Larry's lips as he sat down beside Dani. "She would've been so proud of the person you've become, Dani. And I want you to know that she'll always be with you, even though she's not physically here."

With a sense of reverence, Dani opened the journal, flipping through its pages, filled with her mother's dreams and desires. As she read the words, a surge of connection flowed through her. It was as if she was getting to know her mother in a way she hadn't before.

Larry's voice broke the silence, filled with warmth and love. "Your mother always believed in following your dreams, Dani. She believed in taking risks, learning from mistakes, and embracing the beauty of life's unpredictable journey. As you embark on this new chapter, I want you to carry her spirit within you."

A tear slipped down Dani's cheek as she closed the journal, holding it close to her heart. "Thank you, Dad. This means more to me than I can say."

Larry reached out, gently wiping away her tear, his voice filled with tenderness. "You're my greatest joy, Dani. And as you go forth, know that my love and support will be with you every step of the way. Whenever you need me, I'll be here."

As they held each other, a sense of peace settled upon them. Larry and Dani shared a profound understanding, a connection that transcended words. In this moment of vulnerability and love, they forged a memory that would sustain them through the challenges that lay ahead.

And so, with hearts filled with love and hope, father and daughter embarked on their respective journeys, knowing that their bond would endure, anchoring them in the face of life's uncertainties.

¤

Larry was awakened by Farley before dawn. She kissed his

forehead. He swiftly moved to wrap his arms around her, but she squirmed away before he could reach her.

"Good morning, Sir," she said, amused by his spontaneous gesture of affection. "We have a long day today. I suggest that you stretch and eat a hearty breakfast today before we resume the examination."

"What makes today special?" Larry asked.

"Each subsequent evaluation evolves from the results of each previous session. Every test will be more challenging than the last, bringing in additional aspects of your mental and physical selves to confront you with. Yesterday was a warm up. Today, it goes to the next level. But first, you need to be limber and fueled before you return to the Overlords' examination program."

She rose from the bed. She was already wearing a sports bra and bike shorts.

"Get dressed and meet me in the living room in 5 minutes!"

Larry groaned, rubbing his eyes to shake off the remnants of sleep. Swinging his legs over the bed's edge, he stretched, his arms reaching above his head as he eased the soreness of his injuries and the stiffness from the previous day's examinations. As he reached for his clothes, he couldn't help but wonder what awaited him in the next round of evaluations.

Larry changed into his favorite pair of dark blue running shorts and bright yellow t-shirt. He stumbled into the living room and found Farley waiting. She had already spread out two purple mats side by side and motioned for Larry to join her.

With a deep breath, Larry settled into the mat beside her, carefully mirroring her movements as they began their warm-up. Larry's limbs grew lighter and more agile as they went through the routine. He experienced a surge of adrenaline that pushed him beyond what he believed was achievable given his condition.

Farley spoke between stretches, her words pushing Larry to keep going. "The Overlords believe that true progress can only be achieved by pushing beyond our known limits," she said. "These evaluations are their way of determining who can rise to the challenges that lie ahead."

Larry nodded in understanding before joining Farley for a demanding workout that tested his strength, agility, and endurance. Sweat glistened on both their bodies as they pushed themselves past their limits. All the while, Larry marveled at Farley's own physical prowess; she effortlessly demonstrated each move with such strength and grace.

Throughout the training session, Farley pushed Larry to his limits, urging him to dig deeper, to find the reserves of energy and determination within himself. Despite the physical strain, Larry felt a growing sense of accomplishment and resilience with each rep, each push-up, each sprint.

"OK," Farley said between quick breaths. "I think that's enough stretching. She retrieved the bottle with the integral straw from the kitchen counter and handed it to Larry. "Drink it all."

Larry took the bottle and sucked it down. This time, the liquid had a sweet, slightly acidic taste that was mildly unpleasant. He slowed his drinking in response.

"All of it!" Farley commanded, tilting the bottle in his hand to force the flow to increase.

When Larry finished the contents of the bottle, he groaned.

"That tasted like week old Tcho food."

"You'll be thankful that you drank it. Let's go to the bedroom and start your next session with the Overlords."

"You mean that wasn't part of the examination?!" Farley grinned and walked into the bedroom.

¤

Farley gestured towards Larry's desk chair, and he settled into it once again. She carefully strapped his arms and legs, ensuring that the restraints were secure and tight.

"There's a new aspect to today's session," she announced, taking a seat on the bed where Larry couldn't see her. "If at any point you feel overwhelmed, if it becomes too much, simply say 'scrub.' I will hear it, and the evaluation will be suspended."

Larry furrowed his brow, contemplating her words. "And that will end the examination?"

"No," Farley clarified. "You are allowed to 'scrub' once per day. However, if you choose to scrub again, it will be taken into consideration regarding your suitability for further evaluation."

Larry felt the tightness of the straps on his limbs and saw the worry in Farley's eyes. He knew he was about to confront a physical and mental challenge that could reach levels of unbearable pain. If he reached a point where it truly became too much, he had one chance to halt the proceedings - but he also knew that if he chose to take that option, he would be making a weighty decision.

"We're in this together, Sir," she murmured, her voice filled with reassurance. "I believe in you. Remember, it's alright to test your limits, but it's also alright to acknowledge when you've reached your breaking point. Don't hesitate to use the 'scrub' option if you genuinely need it."

Larry nodded, appreciating Farley's unwavering support. He knew he could rely on her to listen for that word and respect his decision should it come to that. It brought him a sense of relief, knowing he had a safety net even in the midst of this grueling evaluation.

With a final glance at Farley, Larry turned his focus to the desk before him. The room was dimly lit, bathed in a soft glow that enveloped his immediate surroundings.

"Clear your mind and relax," Farley instructed.

As he awaited the start of the examination, Larry took a moment to center himself. He closed his eyes, tuning into his breathing, and tapped into the deep well of determination that had propelled him this far.

¤

Larry cautiously entered the twisting corridors of a complex maze. The walls seemed to move, shifting apart and closing in around him, causing him to feel disoriented and lost. A ominous stillness hung over the maze, occasionally broken by faint whispers that he struggled to make out.

Larry's resolve wavered as he navigated through the maze of mirrors, trying to ignore the familiar faces that appeared before him, all filled with disappointment and disapproval. But he pushed forward, determined not to let these illusions consume him. With each new mirror, Larry saw a different part of himself - his fears, his insecurities, his failures. But he refused to believe them. He continued onward, determined to overcome this mind game and emerge victorious on the other side.

As he cautiously ventured deeper into the maze of mirrors, he noticed subtle reflections and expressions that he had never seen before. Piece by piece, a puzzle began to form within his mind. Each turn of the labyrinth seemed to reveal more about himself, as if the mirrored walls were a gateway to his inner thoughts and emotions.

With each step, the pieces came together, guiding him towards a path that required self-awareness and understanding beyond his conscious comprehension. And as he delved further, the clues became clearer, beckoning him to face his deepest fears and insecurities head-on. He felt a newfound determination burning within him as he followed the echoes of whispered voices, pushing through the chaos and confusion.

Every mirror displayed a different version of Larry, each one reflecting a different aspect of his psyche. But instead of shying away from this revelation, he embraced it. For only by embracing his true self could he break free from this psychological maze and find peace within his own mind.

After a painful eternity of moving through the labyrinth, Larry reached its center. The walls ceased their shifting and became still. In the center stood a pedestal. On top was a mirror, polished to a perfect shine; not a single piece of dirt or dust marred its surface. As Larry approached the mirror, his distorted reflection stared back at him, fragmented by all he had experienced. It seemed as if each crack was a piece of his heart that had splintered off and would never grow whole again.

He hesitated for a moment, unsure of what he would see. But as he looked into the mirror, he no longer saw a reflection marred by self-doubt. Instead, he saw resilience, strength, and a sense of purpose. The maze had tested him, but it had also transformed him.

Larry stared at the rectangular mirror, his reflection gazing back at him from its depths. He reached out and touched a corner of the glass, sensing the untold secrets beneath its shiny exterior. The mirror shattered into countless pieces, and in an instant, the whispers within disappeared. As the shards hit the ground, their fragments rose up and twisted together into a mist that swirled around Larry before dissipating into nothingness. With a final exhale, the maze that had surrounded him crumbled into dust.

Larry stood there, in the silence of his own mind, feeling a profound sense of liberation. The trials had been arduous, the horror haunting, but he had emerged stronger than ever before. He had confronted his inner demons and triumphed over the illusions that had once held him captive.

CHAPTER 6

With a surge of confidence coursing through him, Larry emerged from the virtual world knowing he had overcome the day's challenges and emerged stronger than before.

Farley carefully released the straps, allowing Larry to stand on his slightly wobbly legs. He stretched his limbs, savoring the pleasant fatigue mingled with a newfound vitality. Glancing at the clock, he was taken aback by how much time had passed since they had begun the examination.

"The hours have flown by," Larry exclaimed, a mixture of astonishment and pride in his voice. "I didn't even realize."

"That's a testament to your dedication and focus," Farley responded, her voice laced with admiration. "You completely immersed yourself in the evaluation, giving it your all. I'm truly proud of you, Sir."

Larry's smile widened at Farley's words, grateful for her compassion and belief in his abilities. He approached the next day's evaluations with restored enthusiasm. The taste of the energy drink still lingered on his tongue, a tangible reminder of the physical and mental fortitude he had tapped into. He was ready to face the challenges of tomorrow, eager to delve deeper into the depths of his own potential.

Beside him, Farley stood as a beacon of support and guidance. Her confidence in him bolstered his own self-assurance, and he knew that together, they would navigate the path set forth by the Overlords. Each step would bring them closer to unraveling the true extent of his capabilities.

A feeling of eager anticipation coursed through Larry's veins. The upcoming series of tests called for him to push his limits even more. But he wasn't scared anymore. He had come to view the evaluations as a means of personal growth, an opportunity to become the individual he was meant to be.

"Alright, Adonis," Farley said, a playful tone in her voice. "Time for you to hit the shower."

Larry chuckled, appreciating the lightheartedness amidst the intensity. "You're right, Farley. A refreshing shower sounds like just what I need."

Larry limped to the bathroom, his energy depleted from the day's events. His fatigue didn't diminish his renewed sense of determination and resolve. The warm water washing over him was like a cleansing ritual, purging him of the physical and mental trials he had endured and strengthening him for those still to come.

¤

As he showered, Larry's thoughts wandered back to Dani's initial return from Schola during a break. Her uniform, was adorned with the ribbons and decorations of her achievements. The sight of her standing tall and confident had filled him with .

As Dani walked through the door, Larry's heart skipped a beat. She appeared different, her demeanor distant and guarded. Her eyes, once filled with curiosity and warmth, seemed clouded with a newfound sense of detachment.

"Dani," Larry greeted, trying to mask his concern with a warm smile. "Welcome home. It's good to see you."

Dani's response was curt and detached. "Hello, Dad. It's nice to be back."

Larry tried to engage her in conversation, asking about her studies and experiences at the Schola. However, his questions were met with vague answers, as if Dani was keeping him at arm's length. Larry couldn't help but feel a pang of hurt, the distance between them growing more pronounced with each passing moment.

Over the next few days, Larry noticed a change in Dani's behavior. She seemed immersed in a new ideology, one that alienated her from her family and the values they held dear. The conversations that used to be open and heartfelt turned into tense exchanges, with Dani repeating the beliefs she had been taught.

Larry's worry deepened. The emotional pain of witnessing his daughter becoming so estranged from him and their once strong bond was too much for him to bear. Driven by the desire to mend the widening rift, he proposed a walk in their favorite park to Dani, with the hope of rekindling a more profound bond.

As they strolled along the familiar path, the leaves rustling beneath their feet, Larry mustered the courage to address the growing rift between them. "Dani, I've noticed that you've changed since you started at the Schola. And while I respect your right to develop your own beliefs, I'm concerned that it's driven a wedge between us."

Dani's eyes flickered with a mix of defensiveness and conviction. "Dad, the Schola has given me a new perspective, a broader understanding of the world. I've learned to question the values we've held for so long, to see things in a different light."

Larry took a deep breath, his voice filled with a mix of love and concern. "Dani, I want you to explore and form your own opinions. But I also want you to remember the importance of empathy, understanding, and the love that has always guided our family. We may have different views, but that doesn't mean we can't find common ground."

Dani's gaze softened, a flicker of vulnerability breaking through her guarded exterior. "I didn't mean to push you away, Dad. It's just that the Schola has instilled these beliefs in me so strongly. It's been difficult to reconcile them with what I've known growing up."

Larry reached out, gently placing his hand on Dani's shoulder. "I understand, Dani. Change is a part of life, and it's natural to question and evolve. But let's not let our differences overshadow the love and connection we share. We can learn from each other, respect each other's perspectives, and grow together."

Dani's eyes welled up with tears, her defenses crumbling. She nodded, her voice filled with a mix of remorse and longing. "I've missed you, Dad. I've missed our connection. I don't want our differences to come between us."

Larry pulled his daughter into a warm embrace, tears streaming down his own cheeks. "I've missed you too, Dani. I want nothing more than for us to rebuild what we've lost. Let's embrace our differences, listen to each other, and find a way to navigate this journey together."

In that moment, a glimmer of hope emerged. Motivated by mutual affection and a yearning for reconnection, Larry and Dani committed to reconstructing their relationship through empathy and understanding. They knew that it wouldn't be easy, but they were committed to bridging the gap that had threatened to tear them apart.

And as they continued their walk through the park, hand in hand, Larry and Dani understood that love, patience, and open communication would be the foundation upon which their renewed bond would be built.

CHAPTER 7

When Larry woke, Farley had vanished, and a strange silence filled the apartment and the street outside. With a mixture of curiosity and anticipation, he ventured out of the bedroom, surveying the empty space. The bottle with the integral straw sat on the kitchen counter, catching his attention. Next to it lay a note bearing Farley's familiar handwriting.

The words on the note revealed that Larry would be navigating the day's examination alone. He would need to drink the contents of the bottle when he felt prepared, assume his position in the desk chair, and await the commencement of the evaluation. Farley assured him that she would check in on him later in the day.

Taking a moment to process the situation, Larry's mind swirled with a mix of emotions. There was a tinge of uncertainty, as he had grown accustomed to Farley's presence and guidance. However, he also felt a spark of determination, knowing that this solitary experience would test his resilience and self-reliance.

After a refreshing shower, Larry dressed in comfortable attire, opting for a pair of sweatpants and a soft t-shirt. It was a subtle reminder to find comfort and ease within himself, even amidst the challenges that lay ahead. With a steady resolve, he picked up the bottle and drank its entire contents, adhering to the instructions provided.

This time, the liquid differed in texture and temperature. It flowed thickly, warming his throat as he swallowed each sip. As the liquid made its way through his body, Larry felt a subtle shift in his consciousness. He became increasingly aware of his own presence, as if his spirit was gently detaching itself from his physical form. The surroundings gradually faded away, leaving him immersed in a state of anticipation and readiness.

With a focused mind, Larry embraced the enigmatic nature of the experience and centered his thoughts. He willingly surrendered to the unknown path, immersing himself completely in the present moment. He was prepared to confront the trials and tribulations of the examination, relying on his own strength and resilience to navigate through them.

Larry comfortably settled into his desk chair, finding stability in its familiar contours. With a deep breath, he accepted the solitude, understanding that this experience would challenge him to his utmost and unveil hidden facets of his being.

Time seemed to blur as Larry awaited in front of the laptop for the commencement of the examination. In the stillness of this suspended moment, he found peace, fully present to receive whatever revelations came.

¤

Larry found himself faced with a choice between exposing a corrupt politician who held vital information about the Overlords' intentions or protecting an innocent family who would suffer dire consequences if the politician's secret were revealed. The weight of responsibility bore down on him as he contemplated the implications of his decision.

Larry stood at the precipice of a moral dilemma, his mind spinning with the weight of his decision. The responsibility pressed upon him like a vice. The Overlords had chosen him as their instrument of justice, entrusting him with the power to expose the widespread corruption that had ravaged society. And now, standing at this crossroads, he was forced to weigh the greater good against the lives of the innocent.

If the politician's secret is exposed, it would bring down a corrupt figure and dismantle a powerful network that exploited the weak. It was a tantalizing opportunity to strike a blow against corrupt forces that preyed on society.

Yet, Larry couldn't ignore the faces of the innocent family—their eyes filled with fear and desperation. They were mere pawns caught in a treacherous game, collateral damage in a world where power thrived on sacrifice. Exposing the politician's secret would result in them facing severe consequences and retaliation from the politician's powerful allies.

Doubt's grip intensified, casting a gloom over his tangled thoughts. How could he reconcile the pursuit of justice with the preservation of innocence? Was there a way to navigate this treacherous path without sacrificing one for the other?

In the depths of contemplation, an idea began to take shape—an audacious plan that sought to expose the politician's corruption while simultaneously safeguarding the innocent family. It required a delicate balance of cunning, resilience, and strategic thinking. Larry knew he couldn't do it alone; he needed allies—individuals who shared his desire for justice and possessed the necessary skills to execute the plan.

Carefully, he sought out the shadows, those who dwelled beyond the reach of the corrupt politician's influence. Together, they formed a clandestine network, bound by a common purpose. Farley Lake, a master hacker, Horace Whately, a seasoned investigator, and Gwen Pabodie, a charismatic infiltrator, all brought their expertise to the table, making success more likely.

Larry methodically devised a multi-layered strategy, orchestrating a complex dance of deception and misdirection. His mind was a complex machine, precisely arranging each component to reach its ultimate purpose. He knew that the corrupt politician's web extended far and wide, with powerful allies lurking in every hidden corner. To succeed, he would have to outwit these manipulative forces, exposing their machinations to the blinding light of truth.

The journey was perilous, fraught with treacherous obstacles and unforeseen challenges. Larry's fortitude and adaptability were repeatedly challenged in the face of widespread corruption. Doubts resurfaced like relentless waves, threatening to erode his unwavering resolve. But he drew strength from the innocent faces that inspired him—giving him the courage to press on.

Larry and his team meticulously examined extensive documentation and surveillance footage to expose the politician's intricate web of corruption. Larry, Horace and Gwen gathered incriminating proof and secretly worked to shield innocent families caught in the mess.

As the end of his mission approached, Larry could feel a growing sense of tension in the air. A heavy weight of dread seemed to settle on his shoulders with each step he took, every decision weighed down with immense importance.

Finally, after what felt like an eternity, the moment they had been working towards arrived—the politician's facade of lies was ruthlessly torn away for all to see. As justice was served and truth prevailed, Larry couldn't help but feel a swell of relief in his chest as their mission was successfully completed. The innocent were saved and vindicated, while the guilty faced the consequences of their actions.

¤

As Larry's consciousness reconnected with his surroundings, he became acutely aware of the perspiration that coated his body. The intense experience he had just endured had pushed him to his limits, both physically and mentally. Exhaustion overwhelmed him, weighing down his limbs and sapping his energy. The urgency to attend to his bodily needs arose, but he found himself immobilized, unable to rise from his seated position.

Larry knew he needed to relax, so he closed his eyes and focused on his breathing. The soothing rhythm of his heartbeat lulled him into a deep, restful sleep.

¤

Larry stirred from his slumber, feeling a sense of rejuvenation wash over him. He rose less stiffly that in previous days. Larry showered and ate a simple meal. He wrapped his wounds with fresh bandages and the took his place in the chair before his desk.

He took a deep breath and centered his thoughts on the present, blocking out any distractions and physical discomforts in order to maintain focus. As he cleared his mind, he detached himself from the tangible world and focused on the task at hand: the examination before him. The room fell silent as he delved into a state of deep concentration, his entire being focused solely on the laptop in front of him.

As his consciousness plunged into the depths of the evaluation, Larry embraced the mental landscape that unfurled before him. The challenges, mysteries, and trials that lay in wait beckoned him forward, enticing him to explore the realms of his own potential.

¤

Larry found himself faced with an impossible choice—a situation in which he had to sacrifice his teenage daughter Dani for the salvation of countless innocent lives. The weight of the decision threatened to overwhelm him, his heart torn between loyalty and duty. His mind delved into the depths of his moral compass, searching for a path that would reconcile the irreconcilable.

How did it come to this? How can I choose between Dani and all those innocent lives? It's tearing me apart.

He stood paralyzed by the impossible choice that loomed before him, the air heavy with the oppressive weight of his decision. His daughter, Dani, stood before him, oblivious to the torment that twisted his insides. She looked up at him with innocent eyes, unaware of the harrowing circumstances that now dictated their fate.

"Dad, what's wrong? You seem troubled."

"Oh, it's nothing, sweetheart. Just something I need to figure out."

The knowledge that the fate of countless lives hinged on this decision was suffocating. Every fiber of his being screamed out against the cruel hand that had been dealt to him. Loyalty to his daughter clashed with his sense of duty, leaving him adrift in a sea of conflicting emotions.

"How can I choose between you and all those innocent people? It's tearing me apart, Dani."

"Dad, I don't understand. What's going on?"

He wrestled with the problem, turning it over in his mind from every conceivable angle, yet no matter how he rearranged the options or sought a way out, he couldn't find a solution that wouldn't result in the loss of either Dani or the innocent lives at stake.

"I wish there was another way, Dani. I wish there was a way to protect you and save them, but it seems impossible."

Tears welled up in Larry's eyes as he gazed at his daughter, her smile a painful reminder of the happiness they shared before this dark turn of events. A sense of desperation gripped him, an overwhelming desire to protect her at any cost. But the weight of responsibility crushed down upon him, reminding him that he held the key to countless lives hanging in the balance.

"I love you, Dani. I would do anything to keep you safe, but... I have a responsibility to others too. It's tearing me apart inside."

"Dad, I don't want to see you suffer. We'll find a way, won't we?" she said with tears in her eyes.

Larry accepted the fact that sacrifices were unavoidable in this cruel world. The experience ripped through him, shattering his very essence. He questioned the nature of his existence, the morality of the choices he had made, and the merciless game he had been thrust into.

Larry's voice trembled as he said, "Life isn't fair, Dani. Sometimes we're forced to make impossible choices, and it feels like the world is against us."

Time seemed to stand still as Larry grappled with his decision. The echoes of his daughter's laughter filled his mind, intertwining with the anguished cries of the innocent. His heart was ripped apart; the love for his daughter warred with his responsibility to protect others.

"I can hear your laughter, Dani," he whispered, "but it's drowned out by the cries of others. I don't know what to do."

In the end, Larry knew that whatever choice he made, it would forever stain his conscience. The sacrifice of his daughter would haunt him until his last breath, while the lives he chose to save would be forever tainted by his act of betrayal. There was no escape from the psychological prison that had ensnared him.

"No matter what I decide, I'll carry the weight of this decision forever. It's a burden I can never escape."

With trembling hands and a heavy heart, Larry made his decision, knowing that he could never escape the consequences. He took a deep, shuddering breath, preparing himself for the irrevocable act that would forever alter the course of his life.

"I have to make a choice. It's the hardest thing I've ever done, but it's the only way. Goodbye, Dani."

As the weight of his choice settled upon him, Larry felt a piece of his humanity crumble away. The chamber pulsated with a malevolent energy, as if the very walls bore witness to his agony. The boundaries of his mind blurred, and he descended into a dark abyss of guilt and despair.

"What have I become? How did it come to this?"

Larry's soul was shattered by the psychological horror that

consumed him. The weight of his decision crushed him as his daughter's laughter faded into an endless abyss. In that moment, he was both consumed by guilt and paralyzed by the realization that there was no turning back. He was trapped within the confines of his own choices, tormented by the relentless echoes of what could never be undone. A perpetual conflict between remorse and resignation now defined Larry's existence.

CHAPTER 8

As Larry's senses returned from the examination, he found himself enveloped in the warm embrace of Farley's arms. Her tender hold provided solace, a sanctuary amidst the turmoil that still lingered within him. Tears stained his cheeks, and his body trembled with the aftershocks of the intense experience he had endured.

"Shh, shh, shh. The session is over. You are home now. You are safe and I am here with you."

"It was too real," Larry said sobbing. "It was too vivid. Dani is gone, and it's my fault. I should never have gotten her involved in my work."

"It was predestined. The Oracle of Possibilities tried to get control of her to prevent her from interfering in its release. You were perceptive enough to realize that, and Dani is probably the only reason why we were successful."

"They mutilated her. I didn't even see what they carved into her. And now she is locked away, and I'll never see her again."

"You don't know that. You know that she is at the Schola. Superintendent Gaunt said she would use her leverage to arrange for you to get in contact with her. Have faith in those who support you. Things will get better, eventually."

As he rose from the chair, Larry's legs gave way, and Farley quickly came to his aid, providing him with steadfast support. She guided him to the bed, carefully easing him down onto the soft mattress while gently peeling off his damp, perspiration-soaked garments. Detecting his vulnerability, she undressed and climbed into bed with him, seeking comfort in their shared embrace.

Larry sniffled. "I can't believe this happened. I feel so lost."

"I know, Sir. It's devastating, and your pain is valid. But we will navigate through this darkness."

Larry turned toward Farley. Resting his head on her chest, he found comfort in the steady rhythm of her heartbeat. Farley's hand traced soothing circles on his back, a gentle gesture of love and reassurance.

"Thank you for being here with me, Farley,: he whispered. "I don't know how I would make it through without you."

"You don't have to," she replied, also in a whisper. "I'm here, Sir. I'll support you, no matter what."

As Farley lovingly stroked his head, Larry's breathing gradually steadied. Emotionally drained, he fell into a deep sleep, finding comfort in the presence of his steadfast companion.

Larry awakened, his body entwined with Farley's. He felt her shift as he moved and she pressed herself closer to him.

"How are you feeling?" she asked, turning to face him with a soft smile.

"I feel like my soul has been torn apart and then stitched back together. My mind aches, and my body feels weary, despite being confined to that chair the entire time."

"As I mentioned before, the experiences in the examination are undeniably real," Farley replied gently, her fingers tracing comforting patterns on his arm.

"I understand that," Larry said, his voice filled with a mixture of sorrow and intensity. "Dani is gone, and I can't shake the weight of the consequences from that last trial. It felt so vivid, so raw."

Farley nodded, her eyes filled with empathy. "The Overlords have the ability to tap into your thoughts, desires, and past experiences to create these tests. They have access to parts of your mind that even you may not be aware of. And once the examination is complete, they will have a deeper understanding of you."

Larry sighed, processing her words. "How much more is there to endure?"

"It never truly ends, Sir. It evolves, continuously pushing the boundaries of your capabilities." She paused, reflecting on her own experiences. "As for this examination, I believe you are at least halfway through."

Curiosity sparked within Larry. "How long did your own examination take?"

"It lasted about a week, I believe," Farley replied, her tone reminiscent. "Time seemed distorted, and the experience was disorienting. But I was tested under more controlled conditions, with the stringent discipline expected at the Schola."

Larry's thoughts turned to Dani. "Do you think she went through these tests as well?"

Farley's expression turned pensive. "I cannot say for certain, Sir. The curriculum is ever-changing. Considering she had only six months left before her mandatory service, it's possible she had some form of examination. Although, it's also likely they administer it after the mandatory service now. The details elude me."

"Well, for now, let's put that aside," Larry said, determination flickering in his eyes. "You mentioned I'm halfway through, right?"

Farley nodded, her gaze steady. "Yes, Sir. That's my estimation."

"In that case," Larry said, a playful glint in his eyes, "it's time for a recess." He rolled on top of Farley, their bodies intertwining.

Farley's voice carried a note of caution. "I don't recommend exerting yourself, Sir. You'll been mentally and physically strained for the upcoming tests."

Larry's desire burned too fiercely to be extinguished. With a mixture of longing and desire, he replied, "I understand, but right now, I need this. I need this connection with you."

Farley met his ardor with equal intensity, allowing their desires to mingle and intertwine. At that moment, Larry found a brief peace before the challenges ahead.

¤

Larry's fingers gently traced Farley's stomach as he nibbled on her ear, savoring the closeness they had just shared. Farley pulled away, a playful smile gracing her lips.

"That was intense," Larry admitted.

"Indeed," Farley replied, leaning in to kiss his lips. But before their lips could fully meet, she climbed out of bed, a sense of urgency in her movements.

"We need to get started, Sir. There are strict intervals between examination sessions that we must adhere to. Exceeding these limits could jeopardize our suitability for service to the Overlords."

Larry groaned, the mood swiftly shattered by the reminder of their obligations. Farley had a knack for dousing the flames of passion with cold reality.

"Can't we take a short break? We just shared such an intense moment," Larry pleaded.

"As much as I would love to indulge in more, duty calls, Sir," Farley replied, her voice laced with a mixture of responsibility and determination. "We cannot afford to exceed the examination intervals set by the Overlords."

Larry let out a deep sigh, his disappointment evident in the slump of his shoulders and the furrow of his brow. The constant feeling of being watched and monitored weighed heavily on him, like an invisible hand pressing down on his chest, suffocating him. He couldn't help but feel trapped in this life of constant surveillance and scrutiny.

"It's a necessary part of our commitment, Sir. We must maintain our suitability for service," Farley explained, her voice firm but compassionate. "Come on, let's get our workout done and grab a bite to eat."

Grimacing, Larry hoisted himself out of the bed and got dressed. Farley was already suited up and ready to go, beckoning him to hurry. As they walked towards the living room, Larry felt the weight of their obligations bearing down on his injured body. His hand instinctively went to his side, where the wounds from their last mission were still tender. He yearned for a reprieve with Farley, away from the constant demands of their job. But as her gaze met his and the desire between them simmered, he knew he couldn't shirk their responsibilities.

Larry sighed, torn between his duty and his longing for Farley. "I understand," he said resignedly. "Let's get it over with then."

As they began their training, Larry's body protested. His partner pushed him to his limits, but Larry struggled to keep up. Yet as he fought through each exercise, beads of sweat mingled with his scars and his breaths grew more labored. Despite the pain, a fierce determination surged within him, propelling him to surpass his previous limits. For those fleeting moments, the memories of the cult raid faded into the background as Larry focused solely on pushing himself to new heights.

"You're doing great, Sir! Keep pushing!"

"Thanks, Farley. Your motivation really helps," Larry acknowledged, determination burning in his eyes.

After the grueling workout, they cleaned up and sat down to enjoy a simple meal together.

"You know, despite the interruptions, I'm grateful we have each other," Larry confessed, his voice filled with sincerity.

"I feel the same way, Sir."

"And when we have moments like earlier, it reminds me why we fight so hard. It's for a future where we can have those moments without interruptions," Larry said, his voice filled with hope.

"I believe in that future, Sir," Farley replied softly, her hand reaching out to gently squeeze his.

As they finished their meal, Larry braced himself for the challenges that awaited him. The moments of intimacy and connection had fortified him, reminding Larry of their purpose and the importance of their roles in the service of the Overlords.

"Ready to face the challenges, Sir?" Farley asked, her eyes filled with determination.

"Absolutely!" Larry replied with determination in his voice.

Larry went back to the bedroom and sat in the desk chair, ready to face whatever came next.

CHAPTER 9

The examination enveloped his consciousness. In the cramped briefing room, Larry conferred with his team under the intermittent buzz of fluorescent lights. The atmosphere was thick with tension, the weight of their mission pressing down on him. A holographic display flickered to life, revealing distorted images of the latest victim—a young woman, eyes wide in terror, forever frozen in her last moments.

"Another one," Alan muttered, arms crossed over his chest, his weathered face grim.

"Two nights ago," Farley added, her voice low but steady, scanning the photos with an intensity that could ignite a fire. "That makes four this month."

"Each more brutal than the last," Horace chimed in, his piercing gaze unwavering.

Larry cleared his throat, locking eyes with each member of his team. "We need to move fast. This killer is slipping through our fingers, and the Overlords won't tolerate failure." His tone cut through the murmur of unease.

"We have intel suggesting he's targeting Old Dylath tonight," Alan said.

"Then we apprehend him before he strikes again," Larry said.

Alan nodded, his expression hardening in agreement. Farley's sharp eyes softened slightly. Horace remained stoic, a silent pillar of strength.

"Remember, this isn't just about one man," Larry added. "It's about keeping the balance, maintaining order. It's about doing what needs to be done."

"Let's go," Larry said, his voice a blend of gravel and resolve. As they filed out of the briefing room, the weight of the mission settled on Larry's shoulders. He felt the familiar tug of duty clash with the undercurrent of doubt that plagued him. But now was not the time for hesitation. Now was the time for action—for the Overlords, for Dylath-Leen, and whether he liked it or not, for himself.

¤

The concrete beneath their boots whispered echoes through the labyrinthine alleyways of Old Dylath. Each member's breath formed misty ghosts that dissipated into the gloom. Shadows flickered, dancing with the intermittent neon that fought against the oppressive dark. Larry's pulse quickened; the hunt was on.

"Keep your eyes peeled," Larry murmured into his comm bead. He could feel the adrenaline coursing through him, heightening his senses. This wasn't just another job; it was a race against time.

Farley moved silently beside him, her posture rigid, every muscle coiled for action. Horace scanned the alleyways and side streets with sharp, alert eyes, while Alan lagged slightly behind, watching their back. They were ready, but the weight of the night pressed down like a suffocating blanket.

"Stay close," Larry whispered, his gaze darting to the corners where shadows lurked. The streets felt alive, as if they were being watched. A chill ran down his spine.

A figure emerged from the shadowed mouth of an alley across the street. Tall, gaunt, shrouded in a tattered coat that hung off his frame like the wings of some carrion bird. His movements were erratic, head twitching, hands buried deep in the pockets of his coat as if clutching at secrets sewn into the lining.

"Target sighted," Farley breathed into the comm-link, her voice controlled but laced with tension.

Larry watched the killer pause, head cocking to one side as though listening to whispers only he could hear. A streetlight flickered above, casting a jaundiced glow upon the man's face—hollow cheeks, eyes sunken and gleaming with feverish intensity.

The killer's movements were erratic, pacing back and forth as if agitated by some unseen force. His hands twitched, fingers curling and uncurling as though grasping at air. With each step, he muttered to himself, words slurred and chaotic—a twisted litany that made no sense.

"Unnatural. Must eliminate," the target hissed, a smirk creeping across his lips, revealing yellowed teeth. Larry's heart raced. There was something fundamentally wrong with this man—a predator lurking in the shadows, hungry for blood.

Larry signaled for Farley to cut down the alley to the left and Horace to take the right while he and Alan continued slowly forward.

¤

The shadows of the alley swallowed Larry, each step echoing with a mix of urgency and dread. The world outside faded; it was just him and the target. The serial killer was still pacing, his wild movements growing more erratic as they closed in.

"Careful," Larry warned, voice low and steady despite the chaos tightening around them.

Then it happened. The killer whipped around, sensing Larry's approach. His eyes flared wide, manic and feral. With a guttural growl, he lunged forward, a knife glinting in the dim light.

"CID!" Farley shouted, her voice slicing through the night as she leveled her pistol at the man.

The world erupted into chaos. Alan fired first, a warning shot that ricocheted off the brick wall. The killer stumbled but quickly regained his footing, his attention now fixated on Larry. Time seemed to slow as the man's crazed grin widened, revealing those jagged teeth.

"Must eliminate! Must protect!" he screamed, lunging again, and Larry felt his instincts kick in. He sidestepped, narrowly avoiding the swipe of the blade. The killer's momentum carried him past, and Larry seized the moment.

Suddenly, the killer turned, madness dancing in his gaze. "You don't understand!" he shrieked, voice breaking. "They control everything! The Overlords—"

"Wait!" Larry shouted, raising his hands in a gesture of calm. The team hesitated, confusion rippling through them.

"What do you know?" Larry demanded, eyes locked on the killer.

"Everything!" the killer spat, the knife clattering to the ground as he gestured wildly. "They're watching! You're just pawns in their game!"

The world narrowed to the killer's frantic eyes, and in that instant, the gravity of the situation shifted. The mission slipped from concrete objectives to murky implications.

"Focus, Nodens," he whispered to himself. This mission was about justice, about bringing down a monster. Yet now, the stakes felt twisted, a rope fraying beneath his feet. What if capturing the killer meant exposing the Overlords?

And then it happened. The shot rang out, loud and final, reverberating through the air like a death knell. The killer crumpled to the ground, life extinguished in an instant. A stillness settled over the scene, broken only by the distant wails of sirens approaching—harbingers of the aftermath that would follow.

"Did we... did we get him?" Horace's voice trembled, the disbelief palpable in the air.

"Yes," Larry replied, though he felt anything but victorious. The taste of ash lingered in his mouth, the betrayal of his own principles tightening like a noose around his heart. He had sided with the Overlords—his choice had severed the fragile bond of trust with his team.

"Then why does it feel like I've lost everything?" The question hung unasked between them, a chilling specter that would haunt him long after the echoes of gunfire faded into the night.

¤

"Get the perimeter secure!" Larry barked, urgency slicing through the air. Though experiencing an adrenaline rush, the ensuing silence from his team weighed heavily upon him. Horace stood frozen, eyes wide, disbelief etched across his rugged features. Alan's hands clenched into fists at his sides, dark eyes searching for answers that didn't exist.

"Did you really just...?" Horace's voice quivered. It was barely a whisper, but it cut deeper than any blade could.

"Move!" Larry shouted again, desperation clawing at his throat. He knew they had to regroup, to distance themselves from the scene and the consequences of his actions—but in doing so, he felt something fracture between them, a bond he had fought to protect unraveling before his eyes.

"Was that necessary, Larry?" Alan's tone was measured, but there was an edge, a simmering disappointment that crackled in the air. "We could have taken him alive."

"Alive?" Larry snapped, frustration boiling over. "He was a threat! We had seconds to act—"

"Or you could've thought about it," Alan shot back, his voice rising.

The accusation hung in the air, thick and suffocating. Larry felt the weight of their gazes, heavy with betrayal and confusion. Each heartbeat echoed louder than the last, a reminder that he had irrevocably altered their reality.

"Think about what you've done," Horace said, his face turning pale. "This isn't just about justice for the victims anymore."

"Enough!" Larry's voice cracked, desperation spilling out. He raked his fingers through his graying hair, a futile attempt to shake off the growing shadows of doubt. As the sirens wailed closer, he felt the walls closing in—a claustrophobic panic tightening around his chest.

"Are we supposed to trust you now?" Horace continued, his words laced with disbelief. "You've put us all in jeopardy."

"Trust? I did what I had to do!" Larry's voice faltered. Deep down, he knew the truth; he had sacrificed more than just his integrity. He had traded their trust for hollow loyalty to the Overlords—an exchange he hadn't fully grasped until now.

"Did you even think about what the killer might have known?" Alan's question struck like lightning, illuminating the doubts swirling in Larry's mind. "What if there were other victims we didn't know about? Accomplices? Copy-cats?"

"Stop," Larry pleaded, as guilt washed over him like ice water. What had he done? He had been so focused on following orders, on proving himself worthy of the Overlords' favor, that he had forgotten the commitment he made to his friends—to protect them, to fight alongside them.

"Just... give me a minute," he muttered, his voice barely above a whisper. They were standing on the precipice of something monumental, and he felt the ground shift beneath him, ready to swallow him whole.

As his colleagues exchanged wary glances, Larry stepped away, seeking solace in the chaos around them. Each breath felt heavier than the last, laden with regret and the bitter taste of betrayal.

"Is this who I am now?" The question spiraled through his mind, relentless. He faced the darkness of his choices, the specter of lost friendships looming larger than ever. As he looked back at Horace and Alan, he saw the flicker of hurt in their eyes, the shadow of something irrevocably broken.

And in that moment, Larry knew he would never escape the ghost of his decision—each lingering moment echoing the betrayal, a constant reminder of the man he had become.

CHAPTER 10

A sudden jolt sent Larry reeling, as if the very fabric of reality had shifted beneath his feet. The dark alley blurred, and a disorienting surge of vertigo overtook him. He staggered forward, catching himself against the wall just in time to prevent a fall.

Larry closed his eyes, fighting back the nausea that threatened to overwhelm him. The simulation may have ended, but the aftershocks of the experience lingered, an indelible scar upon his conscience. His breathing slowed as he focused on the rise and fall of his chest, trying to ground himself back in this tangible reality.

Larry's His fingers intertwined, clenched into a fist that rested against his mouth, a silent sentinel guarding the cascade of emotions threatening to spill forth. The fluorescent lights above flickered intermittently, their staccato rhythm mirroring the erratic beat of his heart. Each blink was a shutter closing on the world, each opening a stark reminder of the simulation's torments, so fresh in his mind they might as well have been carved into his flesh.

With deliberate effort, he rose from the concrete bench, muscles protesting with a dull ache that resonated beyond the physical—a manifestation of the ordeal that had battered both body and soul. He paced across the cell, his footsteps echoing, a solitary sound in the void of silence that now enveloped him. The scenario had ended, but its resonance clung to him like the industrial smog of Dylath-Leen, opaque and suffocating.

Larry couldn't shake the vision of Horace and Alan's faces—projected by the evaluation, but no less haunting for it. The trust that once fortified their bond felt as though it were disintegrating, like the ancient facades of Tchotown under the relentless erosion of time and neglect. And though it was all a fabrication, the sting of their imagined rejection seared through him as surely as if their words had been spoken in earnest.

In this moment of solitude, Larry contemplated the path that had led him here, to this nexus of deception and duty. How many more evaluations would he endure before the line between reality and simulation became irrevocably blurred?

¤

Larry awoke with a start, the vestiges of the dream clinging to his consciousness. The sense of isolation was palpable, a specter that would haunt the periphery of his existence, ever present and ever poignant. The simulation may have been a test, a preparation for the trials to come, but the lessons it imparted were indelibly etched upon his soul—lessons of sacrifice, the cost of loyalty, and the price of truth in the shadow-draped world of the Overlords.

He sucked in a breath, the cool air sterile and unwelcoming. Beside him, a shadow loomed—Farley Lake, her silhouette sharp against the blinding backdrop. Her presence was both a shield and a reminder of the barriers now erected between him and the world he once knew.

"Welcome back, Sir," Farley said, her voice as controlled as her posture. "You've been through quite the ordeal."

He shifted uneasily in the chair, painfully aware of the bandages, the physical manifestation of wounds that ran deeper than flesh. His heart pounded with a resurgence of adrenaline, but it wasn't the dream that fueled his fight or flight response—it was the distrust for the woman who stood before him, a living embodiment of the Overlord Authority.

"Feels like more than an ordeal," Larry rasped, his throat dry. "Feels like a betrayal." His gaze struggled to meet hers, veiled under a canopy of uncertainty.

"Your feelings are understandable," she replied, her tone attempting empathy yet missing its mark. "But remember why you're here. You have a purpose, Sir—a duty to the Overlords."

That word, 'duty,' hung heavy in the air between them. It was the chain that bound him, a shackle he had willingly accepted, but one that now seemed to be forged from the very shadows that cloaked Dylath-Leen. He felt isolated, a lone figure standing at the edge of a chasm, his friends and their trust lost in the abyss.

"Horace, Alan... they won't even look at me now," Larry said, the words catching on a choked emotion. "All because I chose the mission over..."

"Over personal bonds," Farley finished for him, her eyes locking onto his. "Larry, you were chosen because you can see beyond attachments. You can do what must be done. And you're nearly finished. Just one last push."

Her hand extended, a lifeline offered in the desolate sea of his doubts. Yet, even as part of him yearned to grasp it, to find solace in the solidarity of duty, another part recoiled. Could he trust her? Was this persuasion or manipulation?

"Nearly done," he echoed, a whisper lost in the expanse of his turmoil. It was a mantra, a flicker of hope that perhaps the end justified the means. But could he endure the examination, knowing the cost?

"Trust isn't given freely in our line of work," Farley continued, her demeanor unyielding. "But trust in this—you are essential, Larry. To the Overlords, to Dylath-Leen, to the greater good."

The greater good—a concept once clear as daylight, now as murky as the smog that perpetually blanketed the city. Yet, as he looked into Farley's unwavering gaze, he found himself nodding, motioning to rise from the chair.

"Alright," he conceded, the weight of his decision settling upon his shoulders like a mantle. "Let's finish this."

"I don't believe you are capable of continuing at this moment. You require rest, Sir."

Larry wrestled with his inner turmoil, the weight of his decision threatening to crush him. Eventually, he begrudgingly gave in, knowing he needed to confront the events that had unfolded before he could move forward with any evaluations. "Fine," he exhaled in resignation, dreading the difficult journey ahead.

Farley's lips curved upwards in a subtle acknowledgment of victory, though whether it was for her, for him, or for the Overlords, Larry couldn't tell. As he stood, his muscles protested, but his resolve hardened. He was close to the end, at the precipice of completing what he had begun.

And with each step towards the final phase of the examination, Larry carried with him the ache of solitude, the ghost of friendships fractured, and the unspoken hope that, in the grand tapestry of Dylath-Leen, his actions would weave a pattern of change, however dark the thread may be.

Farley assisted Larry, holding his arm over her shoulder and leading him to the bedroom. Carefully, Farley helped Larry lay down on the bed. Larry took the bottle from the nightstand, but he didn't seem to notice or care about its contents as he took a large gulp. His mind was elsewhere, slowly calming down. Maybe there was something in the drink that helped relax him. He tried to resist the drowsiness, but eventually, exhaustion took over and he fell into a deep sleep.

CHAPTER 11

Sweat beaded on Larry Nodens' forehead as he tossed in his sleep, the sheets twisted around him like the coiled tendrils of some unseen leviathan. The darkness of his bedroom only intensified the vividness of the nightmare that held him captive.

He was back in Dylath-Leen's desolate streets, but they were eerily empty, a stark contrast to the usual bustle of tormented souls and oppressive patrols. The towering monoliths loomed overhead, casting long shadows that swallowed the ground beneath him.

"Horace? Alan?" His voice echoed off the black stone buildings, returning to him as a ghostly whisper. Silence greeted him, save for the distant hum of the Overlords' machinery.

A figure emerged from the gloom—Horace's large frame silhouetted against the faint neon glow of an alleyway. Behind him, Alan's weathered features came into view, both men approaching with grim expressions etched into their faces.

"Can't trust a man who doesn't know where his loyalties lie," Alan said, his voice a low rumble of thunder amidst the quiet of Little Leng.

"Thought you were one of us, Larry. But you're just another puppet for them," Horace added, his calm demeanor now a mask for the storm brewing within.

Larry reached out, a plea for understanding etched into his gesture, but they turned away, leaving him alone in the serene yet unforgiving beauty of Little Leng's immaculate architecture. As they disappeared into the mist that swirled around the district, a piece of Larry went with them; a fragment of his heart torn away, leaving behind a hollow echo of what once was.

Panic surged through Larry's veins, and he reached out, desperate to explain, to make them understand. But his hands grasped at empty air. They stepped back in unison, distancing themselves from him physically and emotionally.

"Wait!" Larry pleaded, his measured tone shattered by a sense of desperation. "It was the mission; I had no choice!"

Horace removed his hand from Larry's reach, the gesture a clear severance of their bond. "The mission... or your soul, Larry? You sold one for the other. We can't follow a leader who's lost his way."

"Horace, please—" But it was too late. Horace turned away, his broad shoulders now a barrier between them.

Alan spat the cigar onto the cracked pavement, the ember dying out as quickly as their camaraderie had. "Goodbye, Larry." His final words were a death knell to years of camaraderie, a partnership forged in the fires of shared adversity and now extinguished in betrayal.

Larry watched as they walked away, their figures becoming part of the city's shadow, leaving him isolated in the cold embrace of Dylath-Leen. A profound loss gripped him, more paralyzing than any physical wound—the loss of trust, brotherhood, and a piece of his own identity.

¤

Gasping for breath, Larry jolted awake, the remnants of the dream lingering like a foul taste. The disorientation of reality's return was a minor relief compared to the haunting possibility that his subconscious fears might one day materialize.

With dawn still hours away, Larry sat up, rubbing his temples in a futile attempt to dispel the images seared into his memory. The trust of his teammates, the bedrock upon which he had built his resolve, now seemed as fragile as the smog-filled sky above the black city.

As sleep lifted, a heavy sense of potential future regret descended upon him. Horace and Alan's faces haunted the dark corners of his room, and within his mind, where the line between evaluation and reality blurred, Larry knew this internal conflict would not relent easily. It would stalk him, just as relentlessly as any predator from beyond the veil, until he reconciled his actions with the indomitable spirit that had once defined him.

¤

Larry's eyelids fluttered open, the light of the morning sun searing through his grogginess. He inhaled sharply, his ribs protesting with dull throbs that resonated with each breath. His bedroom felt cold, antiseptic, and as his vision cleared, he saw Farley sitting beside him, her silhouette sharp against the white walls.

"Easy, Sir," she said, her voice steady.

He pushed himself to a semi-upright position, ignoring the lance of pain that shot through him. His blue eyes, usually so piercing and alert, now squinted with suspicion as they locked onto Farley's composed face. She was a portrait of calm, dark hair pulled back, black leather collar around her neck, hands folded neatly in her lap—a stark contrast to the turmoil churning within him.

"Farley," he rasped, his throat parched, "why are you here?"

She didn't look away. However, there was a hint of something indiscernible in the depths of her gaze.

Larry's mind raced, recalling the betrayal, the sting of Horace and Alan's disappointment. They had trusted him, and he had chosen the Overlords over them—over everything they stood for. Now, in the wake of his decision, the echo of their severed bond rang hollow in his chest.

Farley watched him with an inscrutable expression, giving nothing away. "You need to focus on recovery," she offered after a moment, her professionalism like a veil drawn across her emotions.

"Recovery," Larry echoed hollowly. He glanced down at the bandages wrapping his arms, reminders of wounds both physical and unseen. "Is that all I am to do now? Heal and forget?"

"Sometimes forgetting is a mercy we grant ourselves," Farley said. It could have been sympathy in her voice, or perhaps just a well-practiced empathy.

Larry scoffed. "No mercy in this." He gestured vaguely around the room, encompassing the distant walls of Dylath-Leen and the ever-watchful eyes of the Overlords. "Only consequences."

He stared at the ceiling, a blank expanse mirroring the void within him. His commitment to the Overlords had cost him dearly—the trust of his comrades, the clarity of his purpose, the warmth of camaraderie. And as he lay there in the silence of his own making, the weight of solitude pressed against him with an intensity that was almost suffocating.

In the end, it was not a serial killer or a mission's chaos that haunted him—it was the reflection of a man he no longer recognized, staring back at him behind distrustful blue eyes.

"It's almost over," she continued, reading his hesitation with an unnerving ease. "You're nearly done."

Larry's gaze flickered to her, catching the faintest glint of empathy behind her steely facade. He wanted to reject it, to push away the hand that was offered to him in the dark. But isolation had gnawed at his edges, leaving him raw, yearning for some semblance of connection—even if it was laced with uncertainty.

"Done?" he echoed hollowly. "Or just beginning?"

"Both," Farley admitted, a rare concession slipping from her lips. "The Overlords demand much, but..." She trailed off, her eyes searching his. "But you're not one to back down. Not from this, not from anything."

Larry felt the weight of her words, their truth anchoring him back to reality. His loyalty had been a double-edged sword, cutting ties with those he held dear, yet it was that same fealty that had propelled him forward, time and time again.

"Horace and Alan," he said after a pause, the names tasting like regret. "They don't understand."

"Perhaps not," Farley conceded. "But understanding isn't a luxury we can afford. Not in Dylath-Leen. Not under the Overlords' watch."

She stood, extending a hand to help him rise. Her touch was firm, grounding. In that simple gesture, Larry found the remnants of his purpose. He took her hand, allowing himself to be pulled to his feet. His body protested, but he stifled the pain, burying it beneath layers of determination.

"Finish the examination, Sir" he stated, the words more for himself than for Farley. It was a declaration, an acceptance of the path he had chosen, no matter how fraught with shadows it may be.

Farley's head moved slightly, and her fingertips followed the outline of the collar that symbolized her commitment to him. "Whatever happens, we'll face it together," she affirmed, silently acknowledging her devotion to him.

Larry straightened his back, the lingering traces of the dream slowly disappearing as he faced the harsh realities of his decisions. He was determined to see this through, no matter what obstacles came his way. After taking one last deep breath, he set in the chair, ready to confront whatever challenges lay on the other side. And Farley, his mysterious and wavering ally, remained faithfully by his side.

CHAPTER 12

The examination appeared around him. The alleyway was obscured by shadows, forming a labyrinth of tangled alleys and deteriorating structures that appeared to extend infinitely into the darkness. A sense of heaviness and distortion permeated the air, as if the fabric of reality itself was warped in this strange realm.

Larry's heart pounded in his chest as he watched his target across the street. Dressed in a long black trench coat, their face hidden by the shadow of a wide-brimmed hat, they emanated an aura of calculated danger. Every step they took was deliberate, every glance they gave held the weight of cunning and deception. As Larry followed their movements, he could feel the tension building, knowing that this encounter would be anything but ordinary.

Larry's grip tightened around his weapon, his fingers trembling with a mix of anticipation and apprehension. He knew that this encounter held the key to uncovering the truth, to unraveling the web of mysteries that had entangled his mind. The target possessed vital information, knowledge that could alter the course of his journey and perhaps even his own existence.

Larry's perception of time slowed to a crawl as he carefully observed, his senses finely attuned to detect the subtlest of motions. The distant sound of footsteps echoed through the alley, a haunting reminder of the city's heartbeat. Shadows danced along the walls, shifting and contorting in an ethereal dance.

And then it happened—a subtle glance, a slight shift in posture. The target's eyes met Larry's, and in that moment, a silent understanding passed between them. They recognized that their paths were meant to cross here.

Without hesitation, the target darted into the maze of alleyways, disappearing from sight. Larry's instincts took over as he gave chase, his footsteps echoing through the narrow corridors. The alleys appeared to be shifting and changing, creating a bewildering maze that could ensnare him.

Whispers danced on the edge of his consciousness, their words a tantalizing mix of truth and deception. Doubts crept into his mind, whispering of the possibility that this pursuit was a fruitless endeavor, that he was merely a pawn in a larger game. But he pushed those thoughts aside, determined to see this through to the end.

As Larry navigated the convoluted maze, each twist and turn fueled his determination. He could sense the presence of the target, their energy growing stronger with every step. The air crackled with anticipation, as if the very fabric of reality quivered under the weight of their impending encounter.

Finally, he reached a dead end, a cul-de-sac nestled within the heart of the labyrinth. The target stood there, their back turned to him, an enigmatic silhouette against the dimly lit backdrop. Larry's breath caught in his throat, his pulse quickening with a mix of excitement and trepidation.

Larry's voice roared out like thunder, electric with anticipation. "It's finished," he bellowed, inching closer to the target, his weapon ready to fire. "No more hiding for you."

The target slowly turned, their eyes blazing with a fire of mischief and something darker. A chilling smirk contorted their lips as they uttered a response, their voice soft yet laced with danger. "Is it really?" they purred, their tone filled with mystery.

Larry snarled, his grip tightening around his weapon as if in warning. "What madness are you trying to cause?" he growled, his voice shaking with unbridled rage. "So many have been sacrificed already—I will not be your next victim."

The target's gaze pierced into him, their smirk widening. "Victim? No no no," they whispered in a malevolent purr. "Think of me instead as an omen; a fragment of the maze that lies within you, an embodiment of the obstacles that await."

Confusion and trepidation stormed across Larry's face as he tried to comprehend the riddle before him. "Obstacles? What do you mean?" he demanded, his voice full of desperation and determination in equal measure.

The target's approach was deliberate, each footfall echoing ominously, their aura a palpable mix of intoxicating charm and chilling threat. "You see, Larry, every step you take is not merely a test of strength or skill; they reflect your innermost truths," they said in a low, raspy voice. "Do you have the courage to face who you are? Will you be strong enough to overcome the darkness that lies beneath?"

Larry's heart raced as he felt his resolve buckle beneath the might of those words. Doubt started to seep into his very core, but he gathered his courage by inhaling deeply. He answered back with a newfound energy, "I'll uncover the truth, no matter what lurks in the shadows."

The target cackled maniacally, their menacing laughter lingering in the air. "Ah, the determined hero," they said with mocking glee. "But beware Larry, for if you learn the truth about yourself, it may forever change you."

Silence hung between them like an impenetrable wall before Larry finally spoke again. "I'm prepared for whatever awaits me," he vowed without hesitation, his voice strong and confident.

The target's smile transformed into a sinister grin. "Then proceed, brave seeker," they whispered, their voice a chilling echo in the stillness. "Proceed and uncover the depths of your own psyche. Embrace the terror that awaits."

With that, the target vanished, leaving Larry standing alone in the desolate cul-de-sac.

¤

Farley's voice pierced through the fog in Larry's mind as she leaned on his desk, her fingers directing a straw into his mouth. He gulped down the liquid she offered and noticed the dull ache in his head. "How are you doing, sir?" she asked, concern etched

"Strange as ever," he replied, his voice muffled by the straw, "but I'm fine."

"Are you ready to continue?" Farley asked with concern in her eyes.

Larry paused for a moment, his gaze meeting Farley's. "Why don't you restrain me anymore?" he asked, with a curious tone.

"You haven't shown the need for it. Do you want me to?" Farley offered, ready to accommodate his request.

A grin spread across Larry's face. "That's my job, isn't it? With you," he teased, his voice filled with playful banter.

"Not today, Sir," Farley replied, shaking her head gently. She held out the straw once again, offering him another drink.

Larry obliged, taking a few more sips of the thick brown liquid. The taste was strange yet oddly comforting.

"Let's continue," Larry finally said with determination.

Farley nodded, her expression serious. "Remember that the consequences of your actions within the examination are very real. Any injuries or traumas you experience will carry over when you emerge from the testing. So, please be careful."

"I understand," Larry acknowledged, his tone turning solemn. "No action movie stunts this time."

Farley gave him a reassuring nod, acknowledging his commitment to caution.

¤

Larry stood at the center of a desolate battleground, his feet sinking into the cracked and barren earth. The landscape was a bleak and haunting sight, with remnants of past conflicts littering the ground. The air reeked of sulfur and death, a reminder of the countless lives lost in this cursed place. Bones and rusted armor lay scattered about like forgotten relics, their presence adding to the sense of despair that hung over the area. Jagged rocks protruded from the ground, creating a treacherous path for anyone who dared to venture further into this forsaken land.

As Larry surveyed his surroundings, a sense of unease settled deep within him. The battleground seemed to pulse with an ominous energy, as if it held the secrets of ancient horrors. He could almost hear the echoes of distant cries and the clash of weapons, haunting melodies of past battles that reverberated through the air.

From the shadows emerged the first combat encounter—an abomination forged from nightmares. Its form twisted and warped, a grotesque fusion of flesh and bone. Jagged spikes sprouted from its colossal frame, while its eyes glowed with a menacing fire, reflecting a hunger for destruction. Towering over Larry, it exuded an aura of malevolence that sent shivers down his spine.

Larry's heart raced, his palms clammy with sweat. Fear clawed at the edges of his mind, urging him to retreat, to save himself from the imminent danger. But deep down, he knew that escape was not an option. The weight of responsibility pressed upon his shoulders, reminding him of the innocent lives at stake.

With a trembling hand, Larry gripped his weapon, its hilt cold and reassuring. The polished steel gleamed in the pale light, a glimmer of hope in this dark abyss. Determination welled up within him, overriding the fear that threatened to consume him. He would face this abomination head-on, for the sake of all those who depended on him.

As the creature lunged forward, its claws slashing through the air with lethal precision, time seemed to slow. Larry's senses sharpened, his focus narrowing to every minute detail. He maneuvered, evading the creature's attacks with precision and quick reflexes.

The sound of steel against armored skin reverberated through the battlefield, a symphony of violence and survival. Larry's muscles strained as he unleashed a series of strikes, his weapon cutting through the abomination's defenses. Each blow held a mix of desperation and resolve, fueled by the knowledge that failure was not an option.

Adrenaline surged through his veins, heightening his senses. He could hear the creature's labored breaths, its anguished cries as wounds were inflicted upon its monstrous form. Larry's mind became a whirlwind of strategic thinking, analyzing movements and searching for exploitable weaknesses.

The battle raged on, both combatants locked in a furious exchange of sword blows and parries. Larry teetered between exhaustion and adrenaline. His movements had become sluggish, every swing of his blade taking more and more effort. Still, he mustered the strength to press on, determined to end this dance of life and death.

With one final desperate lunge, Larry thrust his weapon forward, piercing the creature's hide with a sickening thud. They exchanged a lingering glance – Larry's eyes filled with determination, the beast's with shock and fear – before it disintegrated into dust.

He wiped the sweat from his brow and surveyed the damage around him: splintered wooden planks; scorched earth; scattered bones and rusted armor; and an oppressive silence that weighed heavily on his shoulders. He breathed a sigh of relief, proud to have survived another day.

¤

As Larry bent over to catch his breath, the air around him suddenly turned cold and thick. He heard a strange slithering noise and, with a shudder of dread, he looked up. The darkness around him began to swell and part, revealing a nightmare of shapes emerging from the shadows. Tentacles as thick as tree trunks snaked across the ground, their fleshy surface glistening and slick. Larry was approached by a dozen or more grotesque creatures, each one with twisted limbs, eyes, and mouths that seemed to defy nature. Their jagged ridges of teeth protruded from mouths slathered in saliva that sizzled like acid upon the ground.

Hissing and snarling, the creatures filled the chamber with a chorus of terrifying noises, sending unimaginable fear through Larry. The harsh yellow light from their glowing eyes seemed to bore into him, as though they were trying to read his mind and find the weakness in his defenses. He could feel an oppressive force emanating from them as if he were in the presence of something far greater than himself. Their malicious intent seemed to resonate in the air itself, threatening to swallow him up forever.

Larry's heart raced as his breath came in shallow gasps. He felt the familiar thrill of adrenaline and the tightness in his chest that always accompanied it. Sweat beaded on his forehead, and his hands trembled with anticipation.

He tensed every muscle as he watched the approaching storm of enemies closing in on him. He readied himself at the center of the room, his gaze trained on their movements and calculating every possible scenario. He quickly analyzed their weaknesses and thought through all the available options in this life-or-death situation. He knew that even a single mistake could be fatal, and he had to make sure that he made the right decision.

As the creatures advanced, stilted gait and lanky limbs a disorienting blur, Larry acted on instinct. His broadsword struck with cold precision, exploiting the vulnerabilities of their grotesque forms. Sparks flew from his blade as it chipped away at their armor, each hit sending a sickening reverberation through the chamber. His movements were fluid and fearless, though he couldn't help but feel a twinge of revulsion each time his sword made contact with flesh.

The creatures fiercely battled, their claws slashing recklessly in an attempt to cause harm. Larry was pushed to his limits as he weaved around their attacks, executing deft dodges and parrying incoming blows. He had no time to think, only react, moving with a grace born from desperation as he sought to survive this battle of life and death.

The creatures charged with unmitigated fury, ripping through the air with sharp claws and teeth. Larry leapt back to avoid the flurry of strikes, performing acrobatic maneuvers as he skirted around them. His feet danced upon the ground in a macabre ballet of desperation, dodging and parrying with incredible speed and skill as he sought to keep himself alive.

The chamber was filled with chaos; a cacophony of snarls and cries of pain mixed with the metallic tang of spilled blood. Larry's skin was a tapestry of wounds, each strike leaving its own unique mark on his body as he fought to survive against all odds.

Through sheer perseverance and unyielding determination, Larry fought his way through the swarm. With each fallen creature, he felt a surge of triumph, a flicker of hope that he could overcome the horrors that had haunted him. But even in his victories, a chilling realization settled within him—that he, too, carried a fragment of the darkness he battled, that the line between conqueror and monster was dangerously thin.

As the last creature crumbled to the ground, Larry stood amidst a tableau of carnage. The air hung heavy with a suffocating silence, broken only by the sound of his labored breaths and the echoes of his own inner turmoil.

CHAPTER 13

Larry emerged from the grueling day of testing, his body aching, bloody and battered. With care and attentiveness, Farley led him to the bathroom, recognizing his need for solace and easement. Upon entering the hot shower, they were enveloped in a cocoon of warmth and serenity generated by the cascading water and steam.

As the water cascaded over his tired body, Larry leaned against the shower wall, finding solace in its sturdy support. Farley stood behind him, her skilled hands cleaning the new cuts and abrasions, her fingers soothing his sore muscles, applying just the right amount of pressure to alleviate his pain.

Their eyes locked, an unspoken connection forged through shared experiences and unwavering support. Farley's touch became more than a massage—it carried the weight of understanding, compassion, and unspoken affection.

As the water continued to cascade over them, Larry's gaze drifted down, his eyes tracing the contours of Farley's body. Despite the fatigue that clung to him, a flicker of desire sparked within him, a testament to the strength of their connection.

Feeling his longing, Farley gently turned off the water, their bodies now enveloped in the warmth of the steam-filled bathroom. She carefully extricated herself from Larry's embrace, guiding his hands to the towel she offered.

Larry's touch lingered for a moment longer before he reluctantly released her. His appreciation for her presence was palpable, even in the weariness of his gaze.

With a tender smile, Farley guided him out of the shower, their bodies close but their embrace momentarily interrupted. She held his gaze, conveying a reassurance that they would continue to navigate the challenges together.

Farley sat Larry at his desk chair and bandaged the new wounds received in the evaluation. While less intense than Larry's experience, the examination still resulted in some physical marks. His older wounds were healing despite the mental and physical ordeal Larry had endured.

Helping him into bed, she whispered, her voice a soft murmur, "Rest, Sir. I'll be here, always."

As Larry prepared to rest and recover from the trials of the day, he knew that Farley's presence would be a constant source of strength and comfort. In her, he had found a partner, not just in the horrors they faced, but in the moments of vulnerability and intimacy that bound them together.

¤

Larry was awakened by movement. He opened his eyes to see numerous candles casting the bedroom into a dim, romantic glow. Soft music played as Farley walked out of the bathroom wearing only a black leather collar and matching cuffs.

"You ignited my passions earlier, Sir. But I knew you weren't up for it. You should discipline me again. Now"

Larry blinked, momentarily taken aback by the unexpected turn of events. The candlelight flickered and cast shadows in the room, reflecting the mysterious dance of his conflicting emotions. Farley's boldness both surprised and enticed him, stirring a flame within his own depths.

A mixture of curiosity and anticipation surged through Larry's veins, his weariness fading as he faced this enticing proposition. The soft melody of the music enveloped them, creating an intimate atmosphere that crackled with electrifying energy.

With a hint of excitement in his tone, he replied, "Farley, you've always surprised me, and your intensity is captivating."

Larry rose from the bed, feeling a renewed surge of vitality coursing through his veins. His eyes locked onto Farley's, their depths reflecting a mixture of determination and desire. He approached her with a renewed sense of purpose, feeling the excitement of what awaited him.

As he closed the distance between them, his hands reached out, tracing the contours of Farley's body with a tender reverence. The sight of her wearing the collar and cuffs, symbols of their special relationship, sparked a strong mix of dominance and submission in him.

Farley's eyes sparkled with a mixture of surrender and anticipation, her unspoken consent a testament to the trust they had cultivated over time. She willingly let her cuffs be clipped together and followed Larry's guidance as they engaged in a dominant-submissive dance.

With each stroke, each caress, Larry embraced his role, embodying the dominant force that resided within him. Farley's surrender made him more confident and sparked a dynamic that went beyond the physical.

Larry and Farley's passionate encounter intensified as they explored their desires together. The candlelight flickered, creating shadows that danced on their bodies, representing their complex and intertwined desire.

¤

"Good morning, Sir," Farley said from behind Larry's back.

He turned to face her on the bed, pulling her close with a finger through the ring on her collar and kissed her lips.

"You need to release me so we can get you ready for the examination." Her hands were still cuffed together and tethered to the headboard.

"But I like you just the way you are," Larry said as he caressed her chest.

"We need to get you prepared within the allowed interval. Release me so we can stretch and eat before you have to get started."

"What happens if we just lay here for a while?"

"If we exceed the interval, the examination will begin at the appointed time, but you will be neither physically nor mentally centered. It could have a catastrophic impact on your performance and your final evaluation!"

Larry pulled his finger out from of Farley's collar, a reluctant sigh escaping his lips. The allure of staying cocooned in the bed's warmth with Farley bound by his side, was hard to resist. His mind longed for a few more stolen moments of respite before the demanding examination.

"I know the importance of the examination, Farley," he murmured, his voice tinged with a hint of reluctance. "But can't we linger here just a little longer? A few moments to gather our thoughts and find solace in each other's presence?"

Farley's gaze softened, understanding the conflicting emotions within Larry's heart. "I understand, Sir," she replied, her voice filled with tenderness. "But time is fleeting, and the examination waits for no one. We must seize the opportunity to prepare you fully, physically and mentally."

Her words resonated with truth, and Larry nodded, albeit reluctantly. He knew that delaying the inevitable would only add to the weight of anticipation. With a bittersweet smile, he released Farley's hands and swung his legs over the edge of the bed.

Standing up, Larry's gaze met Farley's, a mixture of gratitude and longing reflected in his eyes. "Thank you for guiding me through all this," he said softly, his voice filled with genuine appreciation. "I couldn't ask for a better partner."

Farley returned his smile, her eyes shimmering with a blend of affection and determination. "And I am honored to stand by your side, Sir," she replied, her voice unwavering. "Together, we will navigate the trials that lie ahead, facing the horrors head-on. You have the strength within you, Sir. I believe in you."

As he made his way towards the bathroom, the sound of running water once again filled the air, serving as a reminder of the tasks that awaited him. Larry took a deep breath, allowing the refreshing sensation to wash over him, awakening his senses and clearing his mind.

He moved with purpose, preparing himself for the examination that loomed on the horizon. A sense of foreboding, heavy with the challenges and unknown terrors to come, filled Larry's thoughts. But he held onto those intimate moments in bed, finding them a source of comfort and strength.

With his preparations complete, Larry took his seat at the desk. Farley leaned on the desk facing him, her smiling face focused on him as he relaxed and centered himself.

CHAPTER 14

Larry emerged in the heart of another empty battlefield, surrounded by a barren terrain that still carried the echoes of past conflicts. Anticipation hung in the air, as though the atmosphere held its breath in anticipation of the upcoming trials.

Larry's boots sank into the scorched earth, the soil beneath his feet cracked and brittle. The landscape stretched out before him, a desolate wasteland marred by the scars of countless battles fought and lives lost. The land was scattered with ruins and abandoned weapons, a grim reminder of death.

Larry stood with his rifle ready, the air thick with anticipation. He scanned the battlefield, looking for signs of movement and trying to anticipate what was ahead. His heart pounded in his chest, a mixture of excitement and trepidation coursing through his veins.

The silence was broken by a hail of bullets, striking the ruins of a nearby building. Larry's training kicked in, and he dove behind cover, adrenaline surging through his body. The distant cries of enemy combatants echoed in the distance, and he knew he had to act swiftly.

With a surge of determination, Larry peered out from behind the debris, his eyes locked on his targets. He moved with precision and purpose, his every movement calculated. Bullets flew around him as he returned fire, engaged in a deadly dance of strategy and skill.

Time seemed to blur as Larry fought his way through wave after wave of adversaries. He ducked, rolled, and took strategic shots, using every bit of his training and experience.

The challenges came in various forms—stealthy snipers hidden in the shadows, close-quarters combat against sword or dagger wielding opponents, and high-stakes decision-making where every choice carried life-or-death consequences. Larry's instincts sharpened, honed by the intensity of the battle, as he navigated the treacherous terrain.

As the trials continued, Larry drew upon not only his physical strength but also his mental acuity. He had to make split-second decisions, assessing risks and calculating the best course of action. The weight of responsibility pressed upon him, but he refused to falter.

Amid the chaos and turmoil, Larry felt a sense of clarity emerge—a deep understanding of his purpose and the impact he could have on the world. The evaluation was not just about his own personal growth; it was about his potential to make a difference, to become a force for change.

With each passing obstacle, Larry's determination grew. Exhaustion threatened, but he kept going, seeking his true potential. The trials pushed him to the edge, but he refused to back down.

Finally, after what felt like an eternity, the battles subsided, leaving behind a battlefield strewn with fallen foes. Larry stood, breathless and covered in dirt and sweat, but with a fire burning in his eyes. He had faced the ultimate test, and he had emerged stronger than ever.

Farley approached, a mixture of pride and concern etched on her face. She embraced him, her touch grounding him in reality. "You did it, Sir," she said, her voice filled with admiration.

Larry smiled, a mixture of exhaustion and satisfaction spreading across his face.

As Larry took a moment to catch his breath, Farley rammed into him, and Larry felt an impact on his chest. Larry pulled Farley behind cover and laid her on the ground.

A red pool in her chest rapidly soaked through her coveralls. She looked up at him, eyes wide open in surprise. She tried to speak, but blood flowed from her mouth with gurgling sounds.

Larry's world came crashing down in an instant. Time seemed to stand still as he knelt beside Farley, his heart pounding in his chest. Panic and grief surged through him, threatening to consume his very being. The battlefield, once a backdrop to his trials, now faded into insignificance as his focus narrowed on Farley's life slipping away.

Frantically, Larry searched for a way to save her, his hands trembling as he pressed against her wound, futilely trying to staunch the bleeding. Tears welled in his eyes, his voice choked with emotion. "No, Farley, please... don't leave me. You can't... not like this."

Her eyes, once filled with life, stared blankly into the distance. The full impact of the situation hit him hard, leaving him crushed by grief. He had lost a comrade, a confidante, and a beloved partner. The battlefield had claimed its toll, snatching away a precious life in the midst of their shared struggle.

As grief threatened to consume him, a burning rage ignited within Larry's core. The pain of loss turned into a strong determination to honor Farley's memory and finish the trials she had prepared him for. She had believed in him, and he would not let her sacrifice be in vain.

With a heavy heart, Larry rose to his feet, his body covered in a mix of Farley's blood, dirt, and his own sweat. He turned his gaze to the battlefield, his eyes filled with a newfound determination. The trials had taken on a new meaning, a mission that extended beyond himself. He would forge ahead, not only for his own growth but also as a tribute to the partner he had lost.

As Larry moved forward, each step was imbued with Farley's spirit, guiding him through the challenges that lay ahead. He drew strength from her memory, embracing the pain and transforming it into a driving force to overcome the horrors that awaited him. In her absence, he would carry their bond, their shared experiences, and the lessons they had learned together.

The once brutal battlefield became a sacred place, Farley's memories fueling his resolve to push his limits and fearlessly confront the unknown.

His gaze lingered on Farley's lifeless form for a moment before Larry's fists clenched, his eyes burning with an inextinguishable rage. He vowed, in a near whisper, "I will not fail," his voice carrying the gravity of his commitment. Farley, I'll do this for you.

And with that, Larry set forth, stepping back onto the battlefield, his heart heavy but his spirit unyielding. Farley's presence remained with him, a constant reminder of the strength they had shared and the purpose that now propelled him forward. The trials were far from over, but he would face them with an unbreakable spirit, fighting not only for himself but also for the memory of the partner he had lost.

¤

Larry emerged from the examination in his bedroom to find the blue tinted face of Superintendent Pazia Gaunt regarding him. She watched him for a moment before offering him the bottle Farley had given him previously. Larry's hands were shaking too much, so she put the straw in his mouth.

Larry took a strong pull from the straw only to discover that the contents were a potent alcoholic beverage. He coughed and bent over as the fiery liquid burned his insides. With his eyes watering, he sat back up and looked to Gaunt.

"Inspector Nodens," she said, "your examination is progressing well. There are only a few more tests before your assessment is completed."

"Where's Farley?"

"Detective Lake is no longer your concern. Focus on your assessment."

Larry's heart sank as Superintendent Gaunt's words echoed in his ears. The absence of any emotion in her voice only intensified his worry. He knew he had to push aside his concerns about Farley for now and focus on the task at hand, as difficult as it was.

Taking a deep breath to steady himself, Larry mustered his determination. "Understood, Superintendent. I will do my best to complete the remaining tests."

Gaunt's stoic gaze held a hint of determination as she nodded in agreement. "Good. Remember, Inspector Nodens, your performance in this assessment will determine your future. We expect nothing less than excellence from our top operatives."

Larry nodded, his mind racing with a whirlwind of emotions. The loss of Farley still weighed heavily on his heart, but he knew he had to compartmentalize his emotions and channel them into his assessment. He couldn't afford to let distractions cloud his focus.

CHAPTER 15

Superintendent Gaunt drove Larry to an unremarkable building in the Leen district. The oppressive atmosphere of the long corridors, with their subdued lighting and institutional feel, heightened his anxiety. They entered a bustling room, dimly lit yet filled with high-tech equipment and monitors. The air crackled with palpable tension, and Larry could feel the weight of anticipation hanging in the atmosphere.

While he prepared himself for the next test, Larry's mind kept circling back to the unanswered questions about Farley's absence. He suspected Superintendent Gaunt was withholding information about the situation. A sliver of doubt urged him to find out what really happened.

But now was not the time for inquiries or doubts. Larry knew that he had to focus on the task at hand—to prove his worth, to demonstrate his skills and unwavering dedication. This was his opportunity to showcase his abilities and earn the trust and recognition of the Overlords.

Pushing aside his reservations, Larry took a deep breath, steeling himself for the challenges that lay ahead. He would navigate this uncertain path, drawing upon every ounce of determination and expertise within him. The time for introspection and seeking answers would come later. For now, he had a test to face, and he was determined to surpass even his own expectations.

¤

Gaunt motioned for Larry to lie down on the table laden with electronic equipment. As Larry took his place, attendants strapped down his head, waist, legs and feet, and placed electrodes on various parts of his body. Readings appeared on monitors mounted nearby.

"Relax and prepare yourself, Larry," Gaunt said. "This evaluation will be a little different than the previous ones." The lights around the periphery of the room went out, leaving only the table illuminated. Then she took a seat in the shadows.

A monitor on an arm was put into position over Larry's face, the blinking dot already present. Larry focused on it and the room faded away.

¤

¤

Larry's mind was a pulsating inferno as he dug deeper into the evaluation, consumed by a relentless desire to unravel its enigmatic messages and unearth hidden secrets. The intricate web of clues seemed to have a sinister purpose, taunting him with an elusive truth that he couldn't resist pursuing. With each code cracked and puzzle solved, his determination and fascination burned brighter, driving him towards a feverish obsession that threatened to consume him entirely.

With each new challenge that came his way, Larry's eyes lit up with excitement. His keen intellect and eye for detail allowed him to uncover hidden symbols and cryptic clues, each one leading him closer to unraveling the web of the sinister conspiracy he had stumbled upon. As he connected the dots and pieced together the fragments, a clear pattern emerged, revealing a dangerous network operating in the shadows.

But there was no time for satisfaction or rest. The puzzles seemed to evolve and adapt to Larry's progress, pushing him further down the rabbit hole. It was as if they possessed an intelligence of their own, responding to his discoveries with even more complex challenges and revelations.

As Larry stumbled upon each new discovery, his heart raced with conflicting emotions. A mix of dread and responsibility weighed heavily on him as he uncovered secrets that held immeasurable power over the lives of others. The urgency to reveal the truth burned within him, but at the same time, he couldn't ignore the potential consequences of doing so. His mind was torn between seeking justice and protecting himself and those who may be caught in the crossfire of dangerous forces.

Larry's mind raced as he meticulously untangled the twisted web of lies and deceit. The pieces finally clicked into place, revealing a shocking truth that made his heart pound with both excitement and fear. He could feel the weight of powerful enemies bearing down on him, but his determination to uncover the whole truth only grew stronger. With each step closer to the final revelation, he couldn't help feeling a sense of satisfaction and pride in his own sharp intellect and unwavering quest for justice.

Larry's determination blazed like a wildfire, raging deep within his core and driving him forward despite the doubts and uncertainties that threatened to consume him. With every step he took, he could feel his heart pounding in his chest and his palms slick with sweat. But he couldn't let fear hold him back - he was consumed by an unquenchable thirst for the truth, willing to risk everything on this perilous quest no matter what dangers lurked ahead.

After the last test, Larry lay on the table in the center of the assessment chamber, exhausted and sweaty. Superintendent Gaunt approached him, her expression inscrutable.

¤

"You have performed admirably, Inspector Nodens," Superintendent Gaunt said, her voice carrying a hint of begrudging respect. "Your skills and determination have been duly noted."

With a nod, Larry sensed a blend of relief and eagerness flowing through his body. He had given it his all, pushing himself to the limits, and now he eagerly awaited the outcome, hoping that his performance had been enough to earn him the recognition and answers he sought.

"Now," Superintendent Gaunt continued, her tone stern, "there is one final task remaining. A meeting with the Overlord Authority Council awaits you tomorrow. They will assess your performance and make their final judgment."

Waves of both anxiety and anticipation washed over Larry, leaving him feeling both nervous and thrilled. The meeting with the Overlord Authority was an opportunity to share his successes and find out what happened to Farley and Dani. It was a chance to uncover the truth.

"You have been assigned quarters where you can go to revitalize yourself. I will collect you in the morning," Superintendent Gaunt instructed.

Following her guidance, Larry was escorted to the room he had been assigned. The space was simple, furnished with a desk, chair, bed, and a terminal. A door in the far wall led to a combined bathroom and shower compartment.

Larry was curious as he approached the terminal, but it only provided limited services such as ordering food and requesting medical assistance. Hungry from his exertions, he placed an order.

Then Larry cleaned himself in the shower. The marks on his face and the multitude of bruises, cuts, and scrapes on his body were stark reminders of the challenges he had faced during the examinations.

Having showered and feeling refreshed, Larry emerged to find a pair of coveralls, folded with precision, on the bed, and he also found a food tray, prepared just for him, on the desk. He dressed himself and then meticulously consumed each bite, appreciating the flavor as he restored his energy.

Satiated, Larry settled down to rest.

¤

Lying on his bed, Larry recalled one evening when, as he and a pre-Schola Dani sat at the dinner table, he cleared his throat, breaking the tension that had enveloped the room.

"Dani, I understand your concerns, but we can't forget that the Overlords have brought stability and order," Larry assured firmly.

Dani looked at her father, her brows furrowed in frustration. "But Dad, at what cost? The Selection, the control, the lack of freedom... How can you defend a system that takes away our autonomy and treats us like pawns?"

Larry leaned forward, his tone becoming more intense. "Dani, you have to understand that the world can be a dangerous place. The Overlords have the knowledge and power to guide us, to prevent chaos and ensure our survival. It may come at a cost, but sacrifices are necessary for the greater good."

Dani shook her head, her voice tinged with disappointment. "But what about the people who suffer under their rule? The ones who are taken without consent, like Mom? Can you honestly say that's justified?"

Larry's eyes softened, a mixture of pain and guilt flickering across his face. "Dani, your mother... It's a painful reminder for me too. But we must understand that sacrifices are sometimes necessary for the betterment of society as a whole. The Overlords may not be perfect, but they have prevented chaos and kept us safe."

Dani's frustration turned into anger, her voice rising as she spoke. "Safe? Is it really safety when it comes at the cost of our basic human rights? Dad, we can't just accept this. We have to question, to fight for what we believe in, even if it means challenging the authority of the Overlords."

Larry's expression hardened, his voice taking on a stern tone. "Dani, be careful with your words. We must be cautious about what we say, who we trust. Challenging the authority of the Overlords can have dire consequences for us and those we care about."

Dani slammed her hand on the table, her voice filled with defiance. "I won't live in fear, Dad. I won't turn a blind eye to the suffering around us. We have to stand up for what's right, even if it means taking risks."

Larry's frustration grew, his voice rising as he tried to make his point. "You're being naive, Dani. The world is not as simple as you think. We live in a complex society, and sometimes tough decisions need to be made for the sake of stability."

Dani stood up abruptly, her voice filled with a mix of anger and disappointment. "I thought you would understand, Dad. I thought you would fight for what's right, for our freedom. But I see now that you're just as blinded by the Overlords' propaganda as everyone else."

With those words, Dani turned and walked away, leaving Larry sitting at the table, grappling with the weight of their disagreement. At that moment, the father and daughter had realized that their different opinions had caused a rift between them, and worried about whether their relationship could recover.

CHAPTER 16

Larry was exhausted when he woke up. He rose from the bed and took a shower to revive himself. After putting on the uniform that had been left for him, Larry went to leave. But the door to his quarters was locked from the outside. A blinking icon on the terminal screen caught his attention—a message awaited him.

Curiosity piqued, Larry sat at the desk and clicked on the blinking icon. Superintendent Gaunt's face appeared on the screen, her presence commanding his full attention.

"Inspector Nodens, you are about to meet with representatives of the Overlord Authority Council regarding your performance in the evaluations. I wanted to give you some advice to help you prepare."

Larry's heart skipped a beat as he absorbed the Superintendent's message. The mention of the Overlord Authority Council in connection with his evaluation sent a shiver down his spine. The locked door added an unsettling layer of mystery to the situation.

Leaning in, Larry focused on Gaunt's expression, searching for insights. Her face revealed a mixture of concern and determination, emphasizing the gravity of the impending encounter.

"The Overlord Authority Council holds great influence and power," she began, her voice measured yet tinged with caution. "Their representatives have meticulously examined every decision you've made and every challenge you've faced during your evaluation."

Larry's mind raced, questions flooding his thoughts. What had the Overlord Authority gleaned from his evaluation? What were their intentions toward him? However, time was limited, and he needed to concentrate on the advice the Superintendent was about to provide.

"They excel in psychological manipulation and strategic maneuvering," Gaunt continued. "Prepare yourself for intense questioning, subtle mind games, and the potential for unexpected twists. They will push you to your limits, testing not only your abilities but also your resilience under pressure."

Furrowing his brows, Larry absorbed her words. He understood the importance of fortifying himself mentally and emotionally for the challenges that lay ahead. The representatives of the Overlord

Authority were formidable opponents, and he couldn't afford to let his guard down.

Superintendent Gaunt's voice lowered, laced with a blend of concern and determination. "Remember, Inspector Nodens, stay true to your convictions. Trust your instincts and don't be swayed by their manipulations. Your integrity is your greatest weapon."

Nodding in acknowledgment, Larry felt a spark of determination ignite within him. He had faced countless obstacles and triumphed over numerous trials throughout his career, but this encounter would undoubtedly test his mettle like never before. Superintendent Gaunt's advice was extremely valuable, keeping him grounded and giving him the determination to continue.

As the screen faded to black, Larry leaned back in his chair, his mind buzzing with a mixture of anticipation and apprehension. The meeting with the representatives of the Overlord Authority loomed before him, promising a battle of wits and wills. But he was ready. He would face the challenges head-on, steadfast in his commitment to uncover the truth and protect those he cared about.

¤

Larry stood with his escort outside the imposing doors of the meeting room, taking a moment to gather his thoughts and steady his nerves. Superintendent Gaunt's words echoed in his mind. The Overlord Authority, an enigmatic and powerful organization, were notorious for their ruthless tactics and unwavering scrutiny.

With a deep breath, Larry pushed open the doors and entered the room. The room was buzzing with anticipation, and the representatives of the Overlord Authority Council sat at a long table, their expressions inscrutable. Approaching, he felt the pressure of their combined gazes, dissecting his every step.

The room exuded opulence, adorned with intricate tapestries and lavish furnishings. It was a stark contrast to the starkness of the evaluation chambers he had grown accustomed to. The surroundings were carefully crafted to project dominance and authority, leaving no doubt as to the Overlord Authority's position of power.

Taking his place at the center of the room, Larry met the piercing gazes of the representatives. Distinctive blue skin and sharp facial features identified them as Overlord-Human hybrids. Their eyes bore into him, radiating intelligence and calculation. He could sense their readiness to scrutinize his every word and action, to test his very essence.

The lead representative, a woman with an imposing air of power, broke the silence. Her loud and authoritative voice echoed throughout the room. "Lazarus Balthesar Nodens, we have diligently reviewed your accomplishments in the evaluation. It is evident that you maintain unparalleled skills and indomitable strength in even the most challenging of circumstances."

Larry's heart raced as he steeled himself for the onslaught of inquiries and tribulations about to come. He had to remain firm in his principles, unyielding in his commitment to what had driven him throughout his career.

As the representative leaned forward, her captivating eyes locking onto Larry's, her voice dropped into a low and forceful tone. "Nevertheless, we are not swayed by outward appearances. This evaluation is a grueling process designed to discover not only your merits but also your weaknesses. We must understand the depths of your soul, your moral fiber, and your capacity for skirting the intricate lines of our world."

Larry's steely gaze met the representative's unwavering stare with fearless confidence. "I am aware of this assessment's gravity," he answered firmly.

A flash of intrigue glimmered in the representative's eyes as she reclined in her chair, granting Larry a faint nod of acknowledgement. "Your record certainly illuminates your devotion and perseverance," she said. "Your actions today, Inspector Nodens, will be carefully considered beyond the documented evidence."

Larry's mind raced, knowing that he needed to provide more than just words. He had to show that he was smart and capable of understanding the complexities of the Overlord Authority's world. With confidence, he continued, "I welcome the opportunity to showcase my adaptability and sound judgment. I am prepared to confront the challenges that lie ahead, to face the tests of character and resilience that await me."

¤

The lead representative leaned forward, her piercing gaze focused on Larry. "Your dedication to absolute obedience is commendable, Inspector Nodens. However, we must delve deeper into your mindset to ensure your unwavering loyalty."

Larry's jaw tightened, but he maintained his composure. "I am prepared to answer any further inquiries," he replied, his voice steady.

Another representative, a man with an air of authority, spoke next. "Inspector Nodens, in your commitment to the Overlord Authority, there may come a time when you face conflicting loyalties or moral dilemmas. How will you navigate such situations while remaining faithful to our cause?"

Larry took a moment to gather his thoughts before responding. "I recognize the possibility of such challenges, and my loyalty lies solely with the Overlords. In those moments, I will trust in the wisdom and guidance of the Overlords, for their motives are beyond human understanding. I will set aside personal sentiments and adhere to their directives, no matter how difficult the circumstances may be."

A representative with a discerning gaze leaned back in his chair, a hint of skepticism in his voice. "Inspector Nodens, true loyalty requires unwavering dedication, even when faced with personal sacrifice. Can you assure us that you will not falter in upholding the authority of the Overlords, regardless of the hardships you may encounter."

Larry's eyes narrowed with determination. "I can give you my word that I will remain steadfast in my commitment. I understand the significance of my responsibility and the sacrifices it may demand. My allegiance to the Overlords surpasses personal concerns or moral dilemmas. I will fulfill my duties with unwavering resolve.

Larry sat back in his chair, his mind racing with the questions posed by the representatives. He couldn't help but wonder why they were so focused on his obedience and loyalty. Were there doubts about his dedication to the Overlords? Or was this a standard procedure for all new members of the Authority?

The representatives continued to ask him more questions, delving into his past experiences and how he handled difficult situations. Larry answered each question honestly, hoping to prove his unwavering dedication.

After what felt like hours of intense questioning, the representatives finally seemed satisfied with Larry's responses. The lead representative stood up, her expression softening slightly as she addressed him.

"Inspector Nodens, your answers exhibit the dedication and conviction we seek in our agents. We will closely monitor your actions and expect nothing less than absolute obedience and loyalty. Remember, any deviation from the path set by the Overlord Authority will have severe consequences."

"We will now adjourn to deliberate," the lead representative said. Then the representatives rose as one and left the chamber, followed by the gallery.

CHAPTER 17

The gravity of the upcoming decision bore down on Larry as he stood alone in the now-empty meeting room. The silence heightened his internal turmoil of doubt and uncertainty. The Overlord Authority Council was all powerful. If they found anything deficient, who knew what might become of him.

With a sudden creak, the doors swung open, revealing Superintendent Gaunt standing in the doorway. Her expression remained stoic and emotionless, offering no glimpse into her thoughts or intentions.

"Inspector Nodens," she began, her voice devoid of any inflection. "You have come a long way since the beginning of our association. I have witnessed your growth, your resilience, and your dedication. Regardless of the result, be assured that you have demonstrated exceptional abilities that few can match."

Larry nodded, a sense of unease creeping into his heart at Superintendent Gaunt's impassive demeanor. "Thank you, Superintendent. I have given everything I had, and I can only hope that it was enough."

Superintendent Gaunt stepped forward, her gaze fixed on a distant point. "You have surpassed our expectations, Inspector. Your journey has not been without its challenges, but it is through those challenges that true character is revealed. Regardless of what lies ahead, know that your efforts have not gone unnoticed."

A mixture of relief and confusion washed over Larry as he absorbed Superintendent Gaunt's words. The lack of emotion in her delivery left him uncertain, questioning the true meaning behind her words.

"I will await the decision with patience," Larry said, his voice determined despite the lingering doubt. "I am prepared to accept whatever fate awaits me."

Superintendent Gaunt's gaze flickered briefly, her features remaining unmoved. "That is expected of you. Your compliance and acceptance are integral to the system."

The gravity of her words settled heavily upon Larry, reminding him of the cold and calculated nature of the Overlord Authority. His hope began to waver, overshadowed by the realization that his fate rested in the hands of an organization that valued obedience above all else.

With a curt nod, Superintendent Gaunt turned and exited the room, leaving Larry to grapple with his own conflicting emotions. The doubts and uncertainties resurfaced, mingling with a deep-seated unease. The evaluation had tested his abilities and loyalty, but it had also exposed him to the unyielding nature of the Overlord Authority.

As he stood there, contemplating the uncertain future that lay before him, Larry struggled to regain his resolve. He was still drawn to the unsolved mysteries of Farley's disappearance, Dani's fate, and the hidden workings of the Overlord Authority.

¤

Finally, the lead representative rose to her feet, her voice cutting through the tense atmosphere. "Inspector Nodens," she began, her tone commanding, "the Overlord Authority has made their decision about your future."

"We are pleased with your commitment and loyalty to the Overlords. You have proven yourself worthy of being part of the Overlord Authority," she said with a slight nod.

A sense of relief washed over Larry as he let out a breath he didn't realize he was holding. He had passed their test and was now officially part of the Overlord Authority.

"As a new member, you will be given access to classified information and resources that will aid you in your duties," another representative added.

But before Larry could fully relax and celebrate his acceptance into the Authority, one final question hung in the air.

"Inspector Nodens, can you tell us your thoughts on those who betray or disobey the Overlords?" asked one of the representatives sternly.

Larry's expression grew stern as he contemplated those who dared to challenge the Overlords. "They are disloyal and must face consequences."

Larry's heart raced, his breath caught in his throat. This moment would shape the trajectory of his life, determining his standing within the authoritarian regime he had devoted himself to.

The lead representative spoke, her words measured and calculated. "In recognition of your unwavering loyalty, exceptional performance, and absolute obedience, the Overlord Authority bestows upon you the rank of Commissar."

Larry felt a rush of relief and pride, pushing away any lingering doubts. His dedication was recognized by the highest levels of authority, proving his worth. The rank of Commissar, with its increased responsibility and authority, weighed heavily on him.

Larry's heart swelled with a mix of anticipation and pride as he absorbed the weight of the representative's words. The significance of his promotion sank in, and he couldn't help but feel a surge of excitement.

The representative's expression remained stoic as he met Larry's gaze. "As a Commissar, you will be granted the authority to make critical decisions on behalf of the Overlords," he explained, his voice carrying an air of authority. "You will have the power to enforce their directives and take actions necessary to quell any threats to the regime's stability. Your loyalty and commitment will serve as an example to others, ensuring obedience and allegiance."

As a Commissar, Larry understood that he would need to exercise sound judgment and navigate the complex web of power and control that governed the regime. With the authority granted to him, he would become an instrument of the Overlords, executing their will with precision.

"I will do everything in my power to uphold the Overlords' will and maintain order," Larry replied, his voice resonating with conviction. I am prepared to take on the responsibilities of this promotion and carry out their directives with dedication.

The representative nodded, acknowledging Larry's commitment. "Commissar, by your actions, you will showcase the power of the Overlords and discourage any challenges to their authority."

A wave of determination swept over Larry. He had come a long way, facing numerous challenges and overcoming personal obstacles to reach this point. With more independence and accountability, he was eager to display his loyalty and determination, regardless of what came his way.

"I understand the weight of this responsibility," Larry affirmed, his voice unwavering. "I will embrace the role of Commissar wholeheartedly, upholding the Overlords' will and ensuring that order is maintained. I am prepared to face any challenges and make the necessary sacrifices to protect the regime's stability."

The lead representative's stern expression softened slightly, a subtle hint of approval in her eyes. "Very well, Commissar Nodens. Your determination and loyalty have been duly noted. May your actions speak louder than your words, and may you carry out your duties with the utmost dedication."

As the conversation ended, Larry was left standing, ready to face challenges and sacrifices for the Overlords.

¤

Superintendent Gaunt's expression remained impassive as she approached Larry and took his hand. She regarded Larry with a calculated gaze, taking a moment before responding.

"Congratulations, Commissar. You are now part of the Overlord Authority," Gaunt replied in a measured tone. "Sergeant Whately and Detective Gilman have proven their loyalty and dedication. They will continue to serve the Criminal Investigations Division in positions suited to their abilities."

"And Farley?" Larry pressed, his voice tinged with concern. "What will happen to her?"

Superintendent Gaunt's gaze flickered, a momentary hint of something resembling sympathy crossing her eyes. But just as quickly as it appeared, her expression returned to its usual icy composure.

"Detective Lake's situation is complicated, Commissar Nodens," Gaunt explained, her voice measured. "She has been taken into custody by the Overlord Authority for further evaluation and assessment. Her fate will be determined based on the information she possesses and her potential value to the regime."

A surge of worry and protectiveness flooded through Larry. He had grown to care deeply for Farley, and the thought of her being subjected to the authority's scrutiny filled him with unease. He knew he had to do something, to ensure her safety and well-being.

"I request permission to speak with the Overlord Authority Council on behalf of Farley," Larry stated firmly, determination burning in his eyes. "I will vouch for her loyalty and dedication to the regime. She deserves a fair assessment, and I am willing to prove her character."

Superintendent Gaunt regarded him silently for a moment, seemingly considering his request.

"Your loyalty is commendable, Commissar Nodens," she said, her tone measured. "But her situation is out of my hands. I am merely a conduit for their instructions to the Criminal Investigations Division."

Larry nodded gravely. He knew that navigating the intricacies of the Overlord Authority's decisions would be a challenge, but he was ready to face it head-on. Dani's well-being and Farley's fate had become his driving force, and he would do whatever it took to ensure their safety.

"Thank you, Superintendent Gaunt," Larry said, his voice filled with resolve. "I will await their decision, and in the meantime, I will prepare myself for the new responsibilities that await as a Commissar."

Superintendent Gaunt offered a brief nod, acknowledging his words. With a final glance, she turned and exited the meeting room, leaving Larry to contemplate the uncertain future that lay before him. As he stood alone, he steeled himself for the challenges to come, ready to face them with a fierce determination to protect those who mattered most to him.

CHAPTER 18

Commissar Lazarus Balthazar Nodens stood before the imposing black stone tower at 500 Klarkashton Avenue, its presence dominating the Downtown district. This obsidian tower, as with all the other towers that appeared when the Overlords arrived, was different and its true purpose was obvious. It was the heart of the Overlord Authority, the seat of power in the city-state of Dylath-Leen.

Looking up at the tower, Larry marveled at its grandeur. The cyclopean entrance beckoned with an enigmatic darkness that concealed the secrets within. There were no windows. Its surface, adorned with countless ancient runes and sigils, bore witness to the mysteries that unfolded within its walls.

As a devoted agent of the Overlords, Larry understood the significance of this place. It was here that decisions were made, orders were given, and the fate of the city was determined. The authority wielded by the Overlords emanated from within these hallowed walls, guiding the lives of every citizen.

For Larry, this tower represented order, stability, and a vision of a better future. The Overlords had brought prosperity to Dylath-Leen, extinguishing the chaos and anarchy that plagued it before their arrival. Under their rule, the city flourished, its citizens protected and provided for.

But deep within his heart, a small voice of doubt whispered. It questioned the cost of this stability; the price paid for the illusion of security. He had seen the fear in the eyes of those who dared to defy the Overlords, the consequences of disobedience that awaited them.

Yet, he had also witnessed the citizens' unwavering loyalty, their blind faith in the Overlords' vision. The city was thriving, and the people had embraced the rules set forth by their enigmatic rulers. To them, the sacrifices made in the name of order were a small price to pay for the peace they enjoyed.

As Larry entered the tower, passing through the archway into the unknown, he couldn't help but wonder what lay beyond those inscrutable walls. What secrets did the Overlords hold? What was their true purpose in choosing Dylath-Leen as their bastion of power?

These questions tugged at Larry's mind, stirring a curiosity that threatened to unravel the very fabric of his allegiance. But for now, he remained resolute, convinced that the Overlords' rule was necessary for the greater good. As he ascended the tower's stairs, he steeled himself, ready to fulfill his duties and defend the authority of the Overlords, no matter the cost.

¤

As Larry ventured further into the tower, he found himself surrounded by an otherworldly landscape that defied human comprehension. The interior was a stark contrast to the familiar structures of the city outside. The black, alien architecture that dominated the space carried an aura of enigma and mystery.

The walls of the corridors were adorned with intricate patterns and symbols, etched in a deep, obsidian hue. They seemed to writhe and pulsate, as if imbued with a hidden energy. The chambers and passages defied any known architectural style, their geometry both mesmerizing and unsettling.

The ceiling soared to heights that seemed impossible, stretching far beyond the limits of human perception. The entire space was bathed in an ethereal, dimly lit glow, casting elongated shadows that danced along the walls.

Structures within the tower defied conventional physics. Floating platforms suspended in mid-air served as walkways, defying gravity's grasp. Staircases twisted and spiraled in impossible formations, leading to destinations that remained hidden from view.

Pulsating orbs of light that floated gracefully in the air, casting an otherworldly illumination on their surroundings. Their gentle glow revealed glimpses of unknown machinery and mechanisms, hinting at the advanced technology that powered the tower.

The tower's immensity dwarfed Larry with each passing moment, making him feel like a minuscule point in an alien expanse. The menacing, dark architecture of the place, with its bizarre design, constantly reminded everyone of the Overlords' absolute power and control. It hinted at a civilization far surpassing humanity's own, filling Larry with awe and a persistent sense of unease.

Within the tower's confines, Larry realized that he was just beginning to scratch the surface of the Overlords' true nature. Their influence extended far beyond the boundaries of Dylath-Leen, and the architecture within the tower was but a glimpse into their enigmatic world. As he continued his journey, he couldn't help but wonder what other secrets this extraordinary structure held, and what awaited him at the pinnacle of the Overlord Authority.

¤

As Larry ventured deeper into the tower, a figure abruptly appeared before him. It was a striking female Overlord-Human hybrid, her presence commanding attention. She had almond-shaped brown eyes and fine, straight, black hair that fell to her shoulders in a smoky hue. Her features were a fascinating blend of human and Overlord characteristics.

"Commissar Nodens," she declared, her voice carrying an authoritative tone. "I am Executor Militsa Hus, your assigned handler within the Overlord Authority. You will address me as Militsa. I will address you by your title to show my authority over you."

Larry pondered Militsa's statement, his curiosity piqued by her explanation. The power dynamics and protocols within the Overlord Authority were far more intricate than he had initially comprehended.

"I see. So, the use of formal titles and familiar addresses serves as a representation of the power dynamics and hierarchy within the Authority. It signifies your control over me as my handler and my submission to your authority."

"Precisely, Commissar. The titles we use and the manner in which we address each other are symbolic of our roles and the structure of the Overlord Authority. It reinforces the authority and control that the Overlords hold over their subordinates."

Larry nodded, absorbing the information. The exchange provided further insight into the subtle ways in which power was asserted and maintained within their organization.

"That's interesting," he said, "because that is the opposite of normal human dynamics. Usually, the use of a title instead of a name implies superiority."

"In our dynamic," Militsa replied, "the use of a title for a subordinate implies an impersonal relationship, while the use of a familiar name by a subordinate for their superior implies dependence."

Larry took a moment to absorb the sight of Hus, her appearance both intriguing and mesmerizing. He couldn't help but notice the revealing, green wardrobe she wore, which accentuated her hybrid features.

"Executor Hus, uh, Militsa" Larry acknowledged, his voice respectful. "It is an honor to meet you."

Hus tilted her head slightly, studying Larry with a piercing gaze. "The honor is mine, Commissar. I have been assigned to guide you through the intricacies of the Overlord Authority, ensuring your seamless integration into our operations."

Larry nodded, feeling a mix of curiosity and apprehension. "I am eager to learn and fulfill my duties as a loyal servant of the Overlords."

Militsa smiled faintly, a glimmer of approval in her eyes. "Dedication and loyalty are valued qualities, Commissar. The Overlords recognize and reward those who serve them faithfully."

Larry straightened his posture, his resolve strengthening. "I will do whatever it takes to uphold their vision and maintain order within their domain."

Militsa acknowledged with a nod. "That is the mindset we seek in our agents. Together, we will ensure the continued prosperity and stability of our city."

As they ventured further into the tower, Hus led the way, guiding Larry through the maze-like passages. Rooms and chambers appeared and disappeared in forms so strange that they were impossible to understand. Some were vast and open, reminiscent of ancient cathedrals, while others were compact and confined, evoking a sense of claustrophobic intimacy. The furnishings and fixtures were equally alien, composed of materials unknown to the human world, with intricate carvings and ornate designs that hinted at a profound knowledge of aesthetics far beyond human understanding. As Larry followed the Executor, she explained the Overlords' instructions and the demands placed on members of the Overlord Authority.

"Your role as a Commissar is vital in maintaining order and upholding the Overlords' vision," Militsa explained with authority. "You will be entrusted with overseeing the enforcement of laws, protection of the Overlords, monitoring of returned Selected, and identifying any threats to the Overlords' rule."

Larry listened intently, absorbing the weight of his responsibilities. The Overlords both impressed and scared him, as he knew their influence went beyond the tower. He was now an agent of their authoritarian state.

"For the Overlords, efficiency, order, and protecting their secrets are paramount. It is our duty to carry out their commands without question."

Larry nodded, his expression focused. "I understand the importance of maintaining the Overlords' trust."

Militsa's eyes gleamed with a mix of pride and expectation. "Good. The Overlords reward loyalty and exemplary service. Your commitment to their cause will not go unnoticed."

As they ventured deeper into the tower, Larry noticed the beings they encountered along the way. Overlord-Human hybrids moved with purpose, their features a testament to the melding of two worlds. Shrouded Lengites, the first encountered by Larry outside Little Leng, performed complex rituals; their chants resonated through the space, generating a surreal atmosphere. Tall Tchotcho clerks carrying various items moved in multiple directions.

"These beings," Militsa said, gesturing towards the diverse occupants of the tower, "are all vital cogs in the Overlords' grand design. Each race brings unique strengths and perspectives, united under the Overlords' overarching authority."

The tower's intricate machinery, a small-scale reflection of the Overlords' control, filled Larry with wonder. He experienced a mixture of awe and apprehension, acknowledging his integration into this sophisticated network and his new role as an agent under the Overlord Authority's direction.

As they walked, Larry's mind swirled with questions. He wondered about the nature of the Overlords, their true motives, and the extent of their control. Deep down, a new seed of doubt began to sprout, but he quickly suppressed it, reminding himself of the importance of loyalty and commitment. Their conversation filled the mysterious corridors as they went further into the Overlord Authority. Larry felt a sense of both anticipation and unease, aware that the choices he would make as a Commissar would shape the course of his allegiance and the future of Dylath-Leen.

CHAPTER 19

Larry followed Militsa through an otherwise unidentifiable wall, leaving him with no choice but to follow, cautiously stepping into the unknown. Upon crossing the threshold, they found themselves within an unusually furnished office.

The office's ambiance matched Militsa's demeanor—cold, emotionless, and devoid of any personal touch. The walls were the same black as the rest of the tower, and seemed to absorb any hint of warmth or color. The ceiling emitted a dim, sterile light, casting a clinical glow over the room. The air felt stale, lacking any discernible scent or hint of life.

It contained minimal furniture. A plain, metal desk stood at the center, free of any clutter or personal effects. A single document rested squarely in the center. Sparse shelves lined the walls, holding a few books and tools, all neatly. The sole item of interest was a simple computer terminal, with its screen showing lines of code in a repetitive pattern.

Militsa's movements were precise and efficient as she approached the desk, motioning for Larry to join her. She silently took the document from the desk—a plain, typed report with no decorations or personal touches.

Larry observed Militsa's detached demeanor, his curiosity now mixed with a sense of unease. He couldn't help but wonder what had led her to this state of emotional detachment and what secrets lay hidden beneath her stoic facade.

As he stood across the desk from her, the room's lifeless atmosphere seemed to seep into his own being, numbing his emotions and dulling his senses. Yet, a small flicker of determination remained within him. He was about to embark on a thrilling journey into the unknown, with the potential to unveil significant mysteries.

¤

Militsa Hus reviewed the document. Once she had finished, she looked up at Larry, her gaze piercing and unwavering. Despite her emotionless demeanor, Larry could sense an underlying intensity in her stare.

"Now, Commissar Nodens," Militsa began in her terse tone, "I want to know more about you." Her words hung in the air, demanding a response.

Larry took a moment to gather his thoughts, aware that he was in unfamiliar territory. He understood the importance of being truthful, even though it meant revealing aspects of his life that he had rarely shared. He took a deep breath and began to answer, his voice carrying a hint of hesitation.

"I've always called Ivy City home," Larry remarked, his voice reflecting his deep connection to the urban neighborhood. "The place was alive with constant motion and vibrant energy, its streets humming with the rhythms of everyday existence."

Larry painted a picture of his diverse urban upbringing, highlighting the various cultures and communities that played a role in his early years. He spoke of the vibrant markets teeming with colorful stalls and the aromatic street food that filled the air with tantalizing scents. The concrete jungle was his playground, its labyrinthine streets his pathways to adventure.

He spoke about his experiences in the city, where he learned to be resourceful and resilient, and his determination grew. "The city taught me the importance of adaptability, as I navigated its complex tapestry of cultures, languages, and social dynamics."

"As I grew older, I witnessed both the vibrant heartbeat and the dark underbelly of the city," Larry revealed, his voice tinged with a hint of introspection. "I saw the stark contrast between prosperity and inequality, the struggle for justice amidst the shadows. It ignited a fire within me—a desire to make a difference, to fight for those who couldn't fight for themselves."

Militsa Hus nodded, her eyes focused and unyielding. She asked pointed questions that got right to the heart of his family history and the relationships that defined him.

Larry took a moment to collect his thoughts, a mix of emotions welling within him as he opened up about his family. "My parents were the pillars of my upbringing," he shared, a touch of warmth in his voice. "They instilled in me the values of resilience and determination. Through their sacrifices, they showed me the true meaning of unconditional love and unwavering support."

Militsa's piercing gaze remained fixed on Larry, her impassive demeanor unchanged. She continued to pry, delving into the dynamics of his immediate family. Larry spoke of his older sister, the bond they shared growing up in the midst of the urban chaos.

"My sister Aurora and I were partners in crime," Larry reminisced, a small smile touching his lips. "We faced the challenges of our urban upbringing together, navigating the streets and creating our own adventures. She was my confidante, my rock during those formative years."

As Larry shared snippets of his childhood, he couldn't help but feel a sense of vulnerability. He spoke of the joys and challenges that had shaped his character, the moments of triumph and the setbacks that had tested his resolve. Each memory shared was like a thread weaving a tapestry of his past, offering Militsa a glimpse into the essence of who he was.

"And where is Aurora now?" Militsa asked clinically.

"She left to fulfill her mandatory service, and I never saw her again." Larry contained his sadness as the memory surfaced.

¤

Militsa Hus's unwavering gaze shifted as she directed her attention towards Larry's daughter, Dani. Larry's heart skipped a beat, his voice tinged with a mix of sorrow and affection as he began to speak about their profound bond.

"Militsa, I... I apologize for the emotional outpouring. It's just that my daughter, Dani, holds a special place in my heart. Our bond is profound, and the memories we shared are etched in my mind with both joy and sorrow."

"I understand the significance of your connection with your daughter, Commissar. However, emotions do not alter the reality of the situation. Could you provide more details about the incident that separated you?"

"Of course. It was during a battle against a cult that worshiped an ancient entity known as the Oracle of Possibilities. Dani played a vital role in our victory, but she suffered grievous injuries. The cultists carved symbols into her flesh, causing her to lose a dangerous amount of blood. The Overlords intervened, just as they did with my wife, Charlotte, years ago."

"The Overlords have assumed control of your daughter, who is now in their custody at the Schola," Militsa stated matter-of-factly.

"Yes, the Overlords took Dani to the Schola. It's become an impenetrable fortress, surrounded by secrecy and bureaucracy. My attempts to reach Dani have been met with resistance and obstacles at every turn. I've used my connections and influence as an inspector, all to no avail."

"Your determination to seek justice and uncover the truth with respect to your daughter is evident, Commissar. But why do you believe it is necessary to learn of your daughter's fate?"

"The circumstances surrounding Dani's custody arrangement, as well as the events that led to it, contain answers that are relevant to both myself and others who have encountered obstacles under the Overlords' regime."

"Commissar, your persistence in questioning the actions and motives of the Overlords is unwise. Loyalty and obedience are paramount in our society, and any doubts or inquiries can be deemed treasonous. The Overlords' decisions are final and should not be questioned. Your focus should solely be on maintaining order and upholding their rule."

"I understand the importance of loyalty," Larry stated, "but when innocent lives are at stake, it is our duty to seek justice and ensure the well-being of those who have suffered. Blind obedience can lead to injustices going unnoticed and unchallenged. We must strive for a balance between loyalty and the pursuit of truth."

"There is no balance to be sought, Commissar" Militsa said sharply. "The Overlords' rule is absolute, and their decisions are made for the greater good. You are no longer a policeman. Your duty is to carry out their orders without hesitation or doubt. The well-being of the collective outweighs any individual concerns, including your personal attachment to your daughter."

"Militsa," Larry said, his voice laced with regret, "I admire your unwavering devotion, but I can't ignore my duties as a father and someone who seeks justice."

"Your continued questioning of the Overlords' actions is futile and dangerous, Commissar. They have guided our society for the better, and it is not our place to challenge their decisions. Your emotional attachment blinds you to the greater purpose. I advise you to reconsider your stance and redirect your efforts towards upholding the Overlords' rule rather than questioning it."

"Militsa, I understand your position, but I cannot turn a blind eye to injustice, even if it comes from those in power. I will pursue the truth and seek justice not only for my daughter but for all who have suffered under the Overlords' rule. If that means risking my loyalty in the process, then so be it."

"Your defiance is noted, Commissar. However, I must caution you against proceeding with such intentions. The consequences of your actions may be severe. Think carefully about the path you choose, as there may be no turning back. The Overlords demand loyalty above all else, and to challenge that loyalty is to invite dire consequences."

CHAPTER 20

Larry continued to stand in the enigmatic office while Militsa looked further into the report before her. The she looked up, face as impassive as always, and continued the interview.

Militsa's voice or tone did not waver as she moved on. "Commissar, as an Inspector in the Criminal Investigations Division, you must have had a team working alongside you. Tell me about the dynamics within your team and the challenges you faced."

"Yes, that's correct. I spent several years at the CID investigating deaths and determining their causes. The primary focus of our investigations was to differentiate between deaths caused by Ravagers and those caused by other factors."

"Can you explain what Ravagers are and how they differ from other culprits?"

"Ravagers are extra-dimensional predators, creatures from another realm that pose a significant threat to our world. They possess unnatural abilities and prey on unsuspecting humans. In contrast, normal culprits are ordinary individuals from our world, who commit crimes due to reasons that are more understandable and relatable to us."

"I see. So, if a death is determined to be caused by a Ravager, it is classified as a Ravager Attributed Death, or 'RAD', correct?"

"Yes, that's correct. When we identified that a death was the result of a Ravager attack, we classified it as a RAD. These deaths are acknowledged and accepted as part of the Overlords' rule and taken over by the Ravager Analysis Task Force."

"What is the role of the Ravager Analysis Task Force?"

"The Ravager Analysis Task Force is a political organization created by the Overlords. Its purpose is to study and analyze Ravager activities, gather data on their attacks, and develop strategies to mitigate the impact of their presence. They aim to soften the impact of the Overlords' rule by putting a more positive spin on Ravager threats."

"And your team at the CID focused on investigating deaths that were not attributed to Ravagers?"

"Yes, precisely. While the Ravager Analysis Task Force dealt with

Ravager-related deaths, my team at the CID handled deaths that occurred within our jurisdiction. These investigations involved determining whether the cause was natural, accidental, or due to normal culprits."

"Thank you for clarifying that. It appears you have experience in dealing with both extradimensional and mundane causes of death. How do you approach these investigations differently?"

"Well, investigations involving Ravagers were commandeered by the Ravager Analysis Task Force. We were cut out of their operations. In contrast, investigations of deaths caused by regular culprits relied on more traditional investigative methods, such as analyzing evidence, interviewing witnesses, and building a case against the perpetrator."

"I see. Your work must have been quite challenging and demanding. How did you handle the emotional toll of dealing with such cases?"

"Emotional detachment is a necessary skill in this line of work. I maintained a professional mindset and focused on the task at hand. While it's important to acknowledge the tragedy of each death, letting emotions cloud judgment could hinder the investigation. I approached each case with objectivity and a determination to find the truth."

¤

"Tell me about the dynamics within your team and the challenges you faced."

"I had a team of dedicated individuals who supported me in our investigations. Each member brought their own strengths and quirks to the table. Gwen Pabodie, our data analyst, was diligent and hardworking, although sometimes a bit ditzy. She had a knack for uncovering patterns in the vast amounts of information we had to sift through."

"I see. And what about Alan Gilman?"

"Ah, Alan was an older member of the team, and he could be a bit grumpy at times. But despite that, he was highly experienced and reliable. Alan always got the job done, no matter the circumstances. He had seen it all and brought a levelheadedness to our investigations."

"And Horace Whately. How did he fit into the dynamics?"

"Horace Whately is an exceptional cop and had been working with me for years. He is reliable, trustworthy, and has a keen eye for details. Horace and I developed a strong working relationship over time, understanding each other's methods and anticipating one another's moves. We were a cohesive unit, complementing each other's strengths and compensating for any weaknesses."

"It sounds like you had a well-rounded team. Can you share some of the challenges you faced during your career at the CID?"

"Certainly. We faced numerous challenges, both in dealing with Ravagers and other culprits. The political interference from the Ravager Analysis Task Force made the Ravager investigations complex. Especially if a case was initially attributed to Ravagers and then found to be of terrestrial origin.

"On the other hand, terrestrial cases brought their own set of difficulties. Some were intricate puzzles, requiring us to connect dots and follow leads through the labyrinth of human motivations. Others were emotionally draining, especially cases involving innocent victims or heinous crimes. Balancing the demands of the job while maintaining our own mental well-being was a constant challenge."

"I can imagine that the job had its fair share of highs and lows. Can you share any particularly memorable moments from your career? Perhaps moments of triumph or cases that still haunt you?"

"There were definitely moments of triumph that made the job worthwhile. Solving complex cases, bringing justice to victims, and uncovering the truth were always satisfying. One memorable triumph was when we successfully apprehended a notorious serial killer who had eluded the authorities for years. It was a significant victory for both justice and closure for the victims' families.

"However, there were also cases that haunt me to this day. Some investigations remained unresolved, leaving behind a sense of frustration and unanswered questions. The memory of innocent lives lost or the relentless pursuit of dangerous criminals can weigh heavily on one's conscience. Those cases serve as a constant reminder of the importance of our work and the need for justice."

¤

Larry completed his account, his voice trailing off as he finished his last response. He looked at Militsa, searching for some hint of emotion or reaction, but her expression remained unchanged. It was as though the information he had shared held no significance beyond its factual content.

Silence settled in the room, the air growing heavy with anticipation. Larry wondered about Militsa's next move and what his journey would be like given her mysterious nature. He was apprehensive and curious as he waited for her response.

Militsa's gaze remained fixed on Larry, her emotionless countenance unyielding to his anticipation. Finally, she spoke, her voice carrying an authoritative tone that left no room for negotiation.

"Commissar, your account has been duly noted. However, it is imperative that you understand the gravity of the situation. Unconditional loyalty to the Overlords is not a choice but a requirement. As a Commissar, your duties lie in supporting and enforcing their rule, not in seeking justice or questioning their decisions."

Larry's heart sank at Militsa's assertion, the weight of her words pressing upon him. He had hoped to develop an understanding, some shared sense of purpose, but it seemed that Militsa's loyalty to the Overlords outweighed any empathy she might have.

"Some of your answers, particularly your belief in the necessity of seeking justice beyond the personal realm, were not favorable. However, I will give you an opportunity to demonstrate your commitment to your assigned duties as a Commissar. Failure to do so would result in unpleasant consequences for you."

Larry's apprehension deepened as Militsa's warning hung in the air, her vague allusions to the potential repercussions leaving his mind awash with concern and uncertainty. Yet, he knew that challenging her further on the matter would only worsen his situation.

"Let it be known that any activities that undermine the authority of the Overlords will be met with severe punishment. You are to proceed with your assigned tasks and responsibilities without question. The path ahead is clear, and it is expected that you will fulfill your obligations diligently."

Though a rebellious spark remained, Larry acknowledged the seriousness of the situation with a nod. He understood the risks he was taking, but his determination to seek the truth and uncover justice for his daughter and others remained steadfast, despite the challenges that lay ahead.

¤

"You may sit." Militsa Hus indicated the chair opposite her.

Larry obediently took a seat, feeling the chair envelop him, its formless composition trapping his torso and legs. He faced Militsa directly, her unwavering gaze upon him.

"I will now explain your duties as Commissar under my direction," Militsa began, her voice devoid of any warmth. "First and foremost, your role is to address matters that are deemed too sensitive for the CID. This includes crimes involving the Overlords, Hybrids, the Selection, and returned Selected. Any cases involving these entities fall under your jurisdiction. Is that clear?"

"Yes, I understand," Larry replied, his voice steady. "As Commissar, I am responsible for investigating crimes related to the Overlords, Hybrids, the Selection process, and the returned Selected. These cases require the utmost sensitivity and attention."

"Your authority is vast, Commissar. You will be granted access to classified information and privileged resources. Your duty is to delve into these cases with meticulousness and discretion. The delicate balance of power within our society relies on it."

Larry nodded, absorbing Militsa's words and committing them to memory.

"I understand the significance, Executor. I will exercise discretion and handle these cases with the utmost care. It is essential to maintain the delicate equilibrium that exists in our society while seeking justice and upholding the law."

Militsa acknowledged his response with a curt nod before proceeding.

"In addition to your investigative duties, you will be required to liaise with other agencies and departments as necessary. Cooperation and collaboration will be vital in achieving our objectives. You will report directly to me and provide regular updates on your progress."

Larry nodded once again.

A subtle shift occurred in Militsa's expression, almost imperceptible, as a glimmer of approval briefly flickered across her features.

"Very well, Commissar," Militsa stated, her voice firm. "You have been given a unique opportunity to serve a purpose that aligns with the Overlords' vision. Remember, your loyalty lies with them above all else. Do not disappoint me."

Larry rose to his feet, brimming with an invigorated sense of duty and determination. He embraced the unexpected twist in his journey, knowing that it would bring formidable challenges. The enigmatic connection he shared with Militsa only fueled his drive to navigate the intricate web of his duties as Commissar, while also uncovering the truth and ensuring justice in a world shrouded in secrecy under the powerful rule of the Overlords. With every purposeful stride, he strengthened his resolve, readying himself for whatever trials might arise on his journey, steadfast in his commitment to unwavering loyalty and obedience to the ruling power.

About The Author

Joab Stieglitz was born and raised in Warren, New Jersey. He is an Information Technology Consultant and also a notary signing agent. He lives in Alexandria, Virginia.

Joab is an avid tabletop RPG player and game master of horror, espionage, fantasy, and science fiction genres.

Joab channeled his role-playing experiences in the Utgarda Series, of pulp adventure novels with Lovecraftian influences set in the 1920's.

You can follow Joab his blog: joabstieglitzbooks.com.

JOAB STIEGLITZ

THE OLD MAN'S
REQUEST

BOOK ONE OF THE UTGARDA SERIES

The Old Man's Request
Book One of the Utgarda Series

Fifty years ago, a group of college friends dabbled in the occult and released a malign presence on the world. Now, on his deathbed, the last of the students, now a trustee of Reister University enlists the aid of three newcomers to banish the thing they summoned.

Russian anthropologist Anna Rykov, doctor Harry Lamb, and Father Sean O'Malley are all indebted the ailing trustee for their positions. Together, they pursue the knowledge and resources needed to perform the ritual.
Hampered by the old man's greedy son, the wizened director of the university library, and a private investigator with a troubled past, can they perform the ritual and banish the entity?

The Old Man's Request is a pulp adventure set in the 1920s, and the first book in the Utgarda Series.

Available in paperback and eBook formats, and as an audiobook

Made in the USA
Middletown, DE
07 February 2025

70332304R00066